Also available in Large Print
by Georges Simenon:

Maigret's War of Nerves

Maigret's Rival

Georges Simenon

Translated by Helen Thomson

G.K.HALL&CO.
Boston, Massachusetts
1988

Published in Large Print by arrangement with
Harcourt Brace Jovanovich, Publishers.

G. K. Hall Large Print Book Series.

Set in 16 pt. Plantin.

Library of Congress Cataloging-in-Publication Data

Simenon, Georges, 1903–
  [Inspecteur Cadavre. English]
  Maigret's rival / Georges Simenon ; translated by
Helen Thomson. p. cm. — (G.K. Hall large print book
series) (Nightingale series)
  Translation of L'inspecteur Cadavre.
  ISBN 0–8161–4426–5
  1. Large type books. I. Title.
[PQ2637.I53I613   1988]
843'.912—dc19   88–1471

—1—

The Evening Local

Maigret surveyed his fellow passengers with wide-open, sullen eyes and, without meaning to, assumed that self-important look people put on when they have spent mindless hours in the compartment of a train.

Well before the train began to slow down as it approached a station, men in large, billowing overcoats started to emerge from their various cells, clutching a leather briefcase or a suitcase, in order to take up their positions in the corridor. There they would stand with one hand casually gripping the brass bar across the window, oblivious, or so it appeared, of their fellow travelers.

Huge raindrops were making horizontal streaks across this particular train window. Through the transparent, watery glass the Superintendent saw the light from a signal tower shatter into a thousand pointed beams, for it was now dark. Farther down, he glimpsed streets laid out in straight lines, glistening like canals, rows of houses that all looked exactly the same, windows, doorsteps, sidewalks, and, in the midst of this universe, a solitary human figure, a man in a hooded coat hurrying somewhere or other.

Slowly and carefully, Maigret filled his pipe. In order to light it, he turned in the direction the train was going. Four or five passengers who, like himself, were waiting for the train to stop so that they could slip away into the deserted streets or quickly make their way to the station restaurant stood between him and the end of the corridor. Among them, he recognized a pale face, which immediately turned the other way.

Old Cadaver!

The Superintendent's immediate reaction was to groan:

"He's pretending he doesn't see me, the idiot."

Then he frowned. Why on earth would Inspector Cavre be going to Saint-Aubin-les-Marais?

The train slowed down and pulled into the station at Niort. Maigret stepped onto the cold and wet platform, and called to a porter:

2

"How do I get to Saint-Aubin?"

"Take the 6:17 train on Platform Three."

He had half an hour to wait. After a brief visit to the men's room, at the very end of the platform, he pushed open the door of the station restaurant and walked over to one of the many unoccupied tables. He then dropped wearily on a chair and settled down to wait in the dusty light.

Old Cadaver was there, at the other end of the room, sitting, as Maigret was, at a table with no cloth on it, and again he pretended not to have seen the Superintendent.

Cavre was his real name, Justin Cavre, but he had been known as Old Cadaver for twenty years, and everyone at the Police Judiciaire used this nickname when referring to him.

He was ridiculous, sitting stiffly in his corner with his constipated air, shifting uncomfortably in order to avoid meeting Maigret's eye. He knew the Superintendent had seen him; that was obvious. Skinny, sallow, with reddened eyelids, he made you think of the sort of schoolboys who skulk peevishly around the playground, although they long to join in the fun.

Cavre was just that kind of person. He

was bright. He was probably the most intelligent man Maigret had come across in the police force. They were both about the same age. Actually, Cavre had a better educational background, and had he persevered, he could well have become a superintendent ahead of Maigret.

Why, even as a young man, had he given the impression of carrying the weight of some curse on his narrow shoulders? Why did he give them all black looks, as if he thought each and every one of them was out to get him?

"Old Cadaver has just started on his novena."

It was an expression often heard at the Quai des Orfèvres some years ago. At the slightest provocation, or sometimes for no reason at all, Inspector Cavre would suddenly embark on a cure of silence and mistrust, a cure of hatred, one might say. For a week at a time he would not say a word to anyone. Sometimes, his colleagues would catch sight of him chuckling to himself, as though he had seen through their supposedly evil schemes.

Few people knew why he had suddenly left the police force. Maigret himself did not learn the facts until later, and had felt very sorry for him.

Cavre loved his wife with the jealous, consuming passion of a lover rather than with the feelings of a husband. What exactly he found so beguiling about that vulgar woman, who had all the aggressive mannerisms of a call girl or a phony movie star, one could only surmise. Nevertheless, the fact remained that it was because of her that he had got into serious trouble while on the force. A story of kickbacks had sealed his fate. One evening, Cavre had emerged from the Chief's office with his head down and his shoulders drooping. A few months later he was known to have set up a private detective agency above a stamp shop on Rue Drouot.

People were having dinner, each in his own aura of boredom and silence. Maigret finished his half-pint of beer, wiped his mouth, picked up his suitcase, and walked past his former colleague at a distance of less than two yards, but Cavre continued to stare down at a patch of spit on the floor.

The little train, looking black and wet, was already at Platform Three. Maigret climbed into a cold, damp compartment of the old-fashioned type and tried in vain to shut the window properly.

People were walking back and forth on the platform outside, and the Superintendent heard other familiar sounds. The compartment door opened two or three times and a head appeared. Each passenger was trying desperately to find an empty compartment. Whenever one of them caught sight of Maigret, the door shut again.

Once the train had started to move, the Superintendent went out into the corridor to close a window that was causing a draft. In the compartment next to his, he saw Inspector Cavre, who this time was pretending to be asleep.

There was nothing to be alarmed about. It was silly to keep brooding on this strange coincidence. The whole thing was nonsensical, and Maigret would have liked to simply shrug it off.

What difference did it make to him if Cavre was also going to Saint-Aubin?

Darkness sped by outside the windows, shot through from time to time with a flicker of light, the headlights of a car, or, more mysterious and inviting, the yellowish rectangle of a window.

Examining Magistrate Bréjon, a delightful, rather shy man of old-fashioned courtesy, had repeated over and over again:

"My brother-in-law, Naud, will meet you at the station. I've told him you're coming."

And Maigret kept thinking obsessively as he drew on his pipe:

"What on earth can Old Cadaver be up to?"

The Superintendent was not on an official case. Bréjon, with whom he had worked so often, had sent him a short note asking him if he would be good enough to pop into his office for a few moments.

It was January, and raining in Paris, as it was in Niort. It had been raining for more than a week, and the sun had not once peeked out. The lamp on the desk in the Examining Magistrate's office had a green shade. While Monsieur Bréjon was talking, and constantly cleaning the lenses of his spectacles as he did so, Maigret reflected that he, too, had a green lamp-shade in his office, but that the one he was looking at now was ribbed like a melon.

"So sorry to bother you . . . especially since it's not a professional matter. Do sit down. . . . But of course . . . A cigar? . . . You may perhaps know that my wife's maiden name is Lecat. . . . It doesn't

7

matter. That's not what I want to discuss. . . . My sister, Louise Bréjon, became Madame Naud when she married. . . ."

It was late. People outside looking up at the gloomy façade of the forbidding Palais de Justice and seeing the light on in the Examining Magistrate's office would no doubt think that serious issues were being debated up there.

Maigret's bulky figure and thoughtful countenance gave such a forceful impression of authority that no one could possibly have guessed at his thoughts.

In actual fact, as he listened with half an ear to what the Examining Magistrate, with the goatee beard, was telling him, he was thinking about the green lampshade in front of him, about the one in his own office, how attractive the ribbed shade was, and how he would get one like it for himself.

"You can understand the situation. . . . A small, really a tiny, village . . . You will see for yourself. . . . It's miles from anywhere. . . . The jealousy, the envy, the unwarranted malice . . . My brother-in-law is a charming person, and sincere, too. As for my niece, she's just a child. . . . If you agree, I'll arrange for you to have a week's leave of absence. My entire family will be indebted to you, and . . . and . . ."

That was how he had become involved in a stupid venture. What exactly *had* the little man told him? He was still provincial in his outlook and, like all provincials, he let himself be carried away by local gossip about families whose names he pronounced as if they were of historical importance.

His sister, Louise Bréjon, had married Etienne Naud. The Examining Magistrate had added, as if the whole world had heard of him:

"The son of Sébastien Naud, you understand."

Now, Sébastien Naud was quite simply a stout cattle dealer from the village of Saint-Aubin, which was tucked away in the heart of the Vendée marshes.

"Etienne Naud is related, on his mother's side, to the best families in the district."

That was all very well. But what of it?

"They live about a mile outside the village, and their house almost touches the railway line — the one that runs between Niort and Fontenay-le-Comte. . . . About three weeks ago, a local boy — from quite a good family, too; at any rate, on his

mother's side, because she's a Pelcau —
was found dead on the tracks. At first,
everybody thought it was an accident —
and I still think it was. But since then,
rumor has it . . . Anonymous letters have
been sent around. . . . In a nutshell, my
brother-in-law is now in a terrible state
because people are accusing him almost
openly of having killed the boy. . . . He
wrote me a somewhat garbled letter about
it. I then wrote to the Public Prosecutor in
Fontenay-le-Comte for more detailed information, since Saint-Aubin comes under the
jurisdiction of Fontenay. Contrary to what
I expected, I discovered that the accusations
were rather serious and that it will be
difficult to avoid an official inquiry. . . .
That is why, my dear Superintendent, I
have taken it upon myself to ask you,
purely as a friend . . ."

The train stopped. Maigret wiped the
condensation from the window and saw a
tiny station, with just one light, one
platform, and one solitary railway man,
who was running along the side of the train
blowing his whistle. A compartment door
slammed shut, and the train set off again.
But it was not the door of the next
compartment that Maigret had heard clos-

ing. Inspector Cavre was still there.

Now and then, Maigret would glimpse a farm, nearby or in the distance but always beneath him as he peered through the window, and whenever he saw a light it would invariably be reflected in a pool of water, as if the train were skirting the edge of a lake.

"Saint-Aubin!"

He got out. Three people in all got off the train: a very old lady with a cumbersome black wicker basket, Cavre, and Maigret.

In the middle of the platform stood a very tall, very large man wearing leather gaiters and a leather jacket. It was obviously Naud, for he was looking hesitantly about him. His brother-in-law, the Examining Magistrate, had told him Maigret would be arriving that night. But which of the two men who had got out of the train was Maigret?

First, he walked toward the thinner one. His hand was already moving up to touch his hat; his mouth was slightly open, ready to ask the stranger's name in a faltering voice. But Cavre walked straight past, haughtily, as if to say, with a knowing look:

"It's not I. It's the other guy."

11

Bréjon's brother-in-law abruptly changed direction.

"Superintendent Maigret, I believe? I'm sorry I did not recognize you right away. Your photograph is so often in the papers. But in this little backwater, you know . . ."

He took it upon himself to carry Maigret's suitcase. As the Superintendent hunted in his pocket for his ticket, he said, steering him, not toward the station exit but toward the grade crossing:

"Don't worry about that."

Turning toward the stationmaster, he cried:

"Good evening, Pierre."

It was still raining. A horse harnessed to a pony cart was tied to a ring.

"Please climb up. The road is virtually impassable for cars in this weather."

Where was Cavre? Maigret had seen him disappear into the darkness. He had a strong desire to follow him, but it was too late. Moreover, would it not have looked extremely odd, so soon upon his arrival, to leave his host standing there and go off in hot pursuit of another passenger?

There was no sign of an actual village. Just a single lamppost about a hundred yards from the station, standing by some tall trees. At this point, a road seemed to open out.

"Put the coat over your legs. Yes, you must. Even with it, your knees will get wet, since we're going against the wind. . . . My brother-in-law wrote me a long letter all about you. . . . I feel embarrassed that he has involved someone like you in such an unimportant matter. . . . You have no idea what country folk are like. . . ."

He let the end of his whip dangle over the horse's rump. The wheels of the cart sank deep into the black mud as they drove along the road, which ran parallel to the railway line. On the other side, lamps threw a hazy light over some sort of canal.

A human figure appeared suddenly on the road, as if from nowhere. It was a man holding his jacket over his head. He moved out of the way as the cart came nearer.

"Good evening, Fabien!" Etienne Naud called, in the same way he had hailed the stationmaster, like a country squire who calls everyone by his first name, who knows everyone in the neighborhood.

But where the devil could Cavre be? Try as he might to put the matter out of his mind, Maigret could think of nothing else.

"Is there a hotel in Saint-Aubin?" he asked.

His companion roared with laughter.

"There's no question of your staying in a hotel! We have plenty of room at the house. A place is ready for you. We've arranged to have dinner an hour later than usual, since I thought you wouldn't have had anything to eat on your journey. I hope you were wise enough not to have dinner at the station restaurant in Niort? We live very simply, however."

Maigret could not have cared less how they lived or what sort of welcome he received. He had Cavre on the brain.

"I'd like to know if the man who got out of the train with me . . ."

"I don't know who he was," Etienne Naud hurriedly declared.

Why did he reply that way? It was not the answer to Maigret's question.

"I'd like to know if he will find somewhere to stay."

"Indeed! I don't know what my brother-in-law has been telling you about this part of the world. Now that he's living in Paris, he probably looks upon Saint-Aubin as an insignificant little hamlet. But, my dear fellow, it is almost a small town. You haven't seen any of it yet because the station is some way from the center. There are two excellent inns, the Lion d'Or, run by Monsieur Taponnier — Old François, as everyone calls him — and just opposite there's the Hôtel des Trois Mules. . . . Well! We're nearly home. That light you can see . . . Yes . . . That's our humble dwelling."

Needless to say, the tone of voice in which he spoke made it abundantly clear that it was a large house, and, sure enough, it was a big, low, solid-looking building with lights showing in four windows on the ground floor. On the center of the façade, an electric lamp shone like a star and gave light to any visitor.

Behind the house, there was probably a large courtyard surrounded by stables, so that one would occasionally catch the warm, sweet smell of the horses. A farm hand rushed up immediately to lead in the horse and cart. The door of the house opened, and a maid came forward to take the traveler's luggage.

"Here we are, then! It's not very far, you see. . . . At the time the house was built, unfortunately, no one foresaw that the railway line would one day pass virtually beneath our windows. You get used to it, it's true, and actually there are few trains, but . . . Do come in. . . . Give me your coat. . . ."

At that precise moment, Maigret was thinking:

"He has talked nonstop."

And then he could not think at all for a moment, because too many thoughts were assailing him and a totally new atmosphere was closing in on him.

The hallway was wide and paved with gray tiles; its walls were paneled with dark wood up to a height of about six feet. The electric light was enclosed in a lantern of colored glass. A large oak staircase with a red carpet and heavy, well-polished banisters led up to the second floor. A pleasing aroma of wax polish and casseroles simmering in the kitchen pervaded the whole house, and Maigret caught a whiff of something else, too, that bittersweet smell that for him was the very essence of the country.

But the most remarkable feature of the house was its stillness, a stillness that seemed to be immemorial. It was as if the furniture and every object in this house had remained in the same place for generations, as if the occupants themselves, as they moved about, were observing special rites, keeping at bay the unforeseen.

"Would you like to go up to your room for a moment before we eat? It's just the family. No fuss."

The master of the house pushed open a door, and two people rose to their feet simultaneously. Maigret was ushered into a warm, cozy living room.

"Superintendent Maigret, my wife . . ."

She had the same deferential air about her as her brother, the Examining Magistrate, the same courteousness, so characteristic of a sound bourgeois upbringing, but for a second Maigret thought he detected something harder, sharper in her countenance.

"I am appalled that my brother asked you to come all this way in weather like this."

As if the rain made any difference to the journey or was of any importance in the circumstances!

"May I introduce you to a friend of ours, Superintendent: Alban Groult-Cotelle. I suspect my brother-in-law mentioned his name to you."

Had the Examining Magistrate mentioned him? Perhaps he had. Maigret had been so preoccupied thinking about the green ribbed lampshade!

"How do you do, Superintendent. I'm a great admirer of yours."

Maigret was tempted to reply:

"Well, I'm not of yours."

He could not abide people like Groult-Cotelle.

"How about serving the port, Louise?"

The decanter was on a table in the living room. The light was soft, and there were few, if any, sharp lines. The chairs were old, most of them upholstered; the rugs were all in neutral or faded colors. A cat lay stretched out on the hearth in front of a log fire.

"Do sit down. . . . Our neighbor Groult-Cotelle is having dinner with us."

Whenever his name was mentioned, Groult-Cotelle would bow pretentiously, like a nobleman among commoners who takes it upon himself to behave as if he were in a salon.

"They insist on setting a place at their table for an old recluse like me."

A recluse, yes, and probably a bachelor, too. You could sense it, though you didn't know why. A pretentious, useless character, quite pleased with himself and his oddities.

The fact that he was neither a count nor a marquis, not even a simple nobleman, must cause him considerable annoyance. Yet he did have an affected first name, Alban, which he liked to hear, and an equally pretentious double-barreled surname to go with it.

He was a tall, lean man of about forty who obviously thought this leanness gave him an aristocratic distinction. The unbrushed look he had about him, in spite of the care with which he was dressed, his spiritless face and bald forehead gave the impression of someone without a wife. His clothes, elegant, their colors subtle, looked as though they had never been new, but also as though they would never become old or threadbare. They were part of his personality, and equally unchangeable. Whenever Maigret met him subsequently, he was always wearing the same greenish jacket, very much in the style of the country gentleman, and the same horseshoe tie pin on a white ribbed-cotton tie.

"I hope the journey wasn't too tiring, Superintendent?" inquired Louise Bréjon Naud, handing him a glass of port.

And Maigret, firmly ensconced in an armchair that sagged beneath his weight, much to the distress of the mistress of the house, was prey to so many different emotions that his mind became rather blunted, and for part of the evening his hosts must have thought him somewhat slow-witted.

First of all, there was the house — the very prototype of the house he had dreamed of so often, with its protective walls enclosing air as thick as solid matter. The framed portraits reminded him of the Examining Magistrate's lengthy discourse about the Nauds, the Bréjons, the La Noues — for the Bréjons were connected with the La Noues through their mother. One would have liked to imagine that all these serious-looking and rather rigid faces belonged to one's own ancestors.

Judging by the smells coming from the kitchen, an elaborate meal was about to be served. Someone was carefully setting the table in the dining room next-door; the clinking of china and glass could be heard. In the stable, the farm hand was rubbing down the mare, and two long rows of reddish-brown cows were chewing the cud in their stalls.

Everything breathed peace, order, and virtue, and at the same time was the very expression of the petty habits and foibles of simple families living their self-contained lives.

Etienne Naud, broad-shouldered, with a ruddy complexion and protuberant eyes, looked cordially around him as if to say:

"Look at me! . . . Sincere . . . Kind . . ."

The good-natured giant. The perfect master of the house. The perfect father. The man who called out from his pony cart:

"Good evening, Pierre . . . Good evening, Fabien . . ."

His wife smiled shyly in the shadow of the huge fellow, as if to apologize for his taking up so much space.

"Will you excuse me for a moment, Superintendent."

Of course. He had been expecting it. The competent mistress of the house always goes into the kitchen to have a last look at the dinner preparations.

Even Alban Groult-Cotelle was predictable. Looking as if he had just stepped out of an engraving, he was the very picture of the superior friend — more refined, better bred, more intelligent, indeed, with his faintly condescending airs, the epitome of the old family friend.

"You see . . ." was written all over his face. "They're decent people, perfect neighbors. . . . You can't talk philosophy with them, but apart from that, they make you feel very much at home, and you'll see their burgundy is genuine enough and their brandy worthy of praise. . . ."

"Dinner is served, madame."

"Will you sit on my right, Superintendent."

But where was the note of anxiety in all this? For the Examining Magistrate had certainly been very concerned when he sent for Maigret.

"I know my brother-in-law," he insisted, "just as I know my sister and my niece. Anyway, you'll see them for yourself. . . . But all this doesn't alter the fact that this odious accusation takes on more substance day by day, to the point of forcing the Public Prosecutor to investigate the matter. My father was the notary in Saint-Aubin for forty years, having taken over the practice from *his* father. . . . They'll show you our family house in the center of town. . . . I am asking myself how such a blind hatred could have developed in so short a time. It is steadily gaining ground and is threatening to wreck the lives of innocent people. . . . My sister has never been very strong. She's high-strung and suffers from insomnia. The slightest problem upsets her."

One would never have guessed, from the looks of it, that the people present were involved in a tragedy. Everything would lead one to believe that Maigret had merely been asked to a good dinner and a game of bridge. While larks were being served, the Superintendent's hosts explained at great length how the peasants caught them at night by dragging nets over the meadows.

But why was their daughter not present?

"My niece, Geneviève," the Examining Magistrate had said, "is a perfect young lady, the like of which you only read about in novels now."

This was not, however, what the person or persons writing the anonymous letters thought, or, for that matter, what most of the local people thought. It was Geneviève they were accusing, after all.

Maigret was still puzzled by the story he had heard from Bréjon, because it was so out of keeping with the scene before him.

Rumor had it that Albert Retailleau, the young man found dead on the railroad tracks, was Geneviève's lover. It was even said that he went to her house two or three times a week and spent the night in her room.

Albert had no money. He was barely twenty years old. His father had worked in the Saint-Aubin dairy and had died in a boiler explosion. His mother lived on an income the dairy had been obliged to give her as damages.

"Albert Retailleau would never have committed suicide," his friends declared. "He enjoyed life too much. And even if he had been drunk, as had been said, he would have known better than to cross the tracks when a train was coming."

The body had been found more than five hundred yards from the Nauds', about halfway between their house and the station.

There was nothing wrong in that, but it was now rumored that the young man's cap had been found in the reeds along the canal, much nearer the Nauds' house.

There was yet another, even more questionable, story in circulation. It seemed that someone had visited Madame Retailleau, the mother of the young man, a week after her son's death, and had seen her hurriedly hide a wad of thousand-franc notes. She had never been known to have such a large sum of money before.

"It is a pity, Superintendent, that you have made your first visit to our part of the world in wintertime. It is so pretty around here in the summer that the district is known as 'Green Venice.' . . . You'll have some more of the chicken, won't you?"

And Cavre? What was Inspector Cavre up to in Saint-Aubin?

Everyone ate and drank too much. It was too hot in the dining room. They all returned to the living room in a sluggish state and sat around the crackling log fire.

"I insist . . . I know you're particularly fond of your pipe, but you must have a cigar."

Were they trying to lull him to sleep? But that was a ridiculous thought. They were decent people. That was all there was to it. The Examining Magistrate in Paris must have exaggerated the situation. And Alban Groult-Cotelle was nothing but a stuck-up fool, one of those dandyish good-for-nothings to be found in any country district.

"You must be tired after your journey. Just say when you want to go to bed."

That meant nothing was going to be said that night. Perhaps because Groult-Cotelle was there? Or because Naud preferred not to speak in front of his wife?

"Do you take coffee at night? . . . No? . . . No tea either? . . . Please excuse me if I go up now, but our daughter hasn't been well for the past two or three days and I want to see whether she needs anything. . . . Young girls are always rather delicate, aren't they? Especially in a climate like ours."

The three men sat around the fire smoking and talking at random. They began discussing local politics; it appeared that there was a new mayor, who was acting counter to the wishes of all respectable members of the community and who . . .

"Well, gentlemen," Maigret grunted finally, half pleasantly, half crossly, "if you will excuse me, I think I'll go up to bed now."

"You must stay the night here, too, Alban. I'm not going to let you go home in this terrible weather."

They went upstairs. Maigret's room was at the end of the hallway. Its walls, covered with yellow cloth, brought back many childhood memories.

"Have you everything you need? . . . I forgot. . . . Let me show you the bathroom."

Maigret shook hands with the two men, then undressed and got into bed. As he lay there half-asleep, he thought he heard noises, the distant murmur of voices somewhere in the house, but soon, when all the lights were out, these sounds died away.

He fell asleep. Or he thought he did. The sinister face of Cavre, that luckless creature, kept creeping into his subconsciousness, and then he dreamed that the rosy-cheeked maid who had served the dinner was bringing him his breakfast.

He was sure he heard the door open gently. He sat up in bed and groped for the switch to the light bulb in the tulip-shaped opal glass covering attached to the wall above the headboard. The light went on, and Maigret saw standing in front of him a young girl with a brown wool coat over her nightgown.

"Ssh," she whispered. "I just had to speak to you. Don't make a noise."

And, like a sleepwalker, she sat down on a chair and stared into space.

—2—

The Girl in the Nightgown

It was a wearying night for Maigret, and yet not without charm. He slept without sleeping. He dreamed without dreaming, or, in other words, he was well aware he was dreaming and deliberately prolonged his dreams, being conscious all the time of noises from the real world.

For example, the sound of the mare kicking her hoofs against the stable wall was real enough, but the other images that flitted through Maigret's mind, as he lay in bed perspiring heavily, were tricks of the imagination. He conjured up a picture of the dim light in a stable, the horse's rump, the rack half full of hay; he imagined the rain still falling in the courtyard, with figures splashing their way through black

28

puddles of water, and lastly he saw, from the outside, the house in which he was staying.

It was a kind of personality splitting. He was in his bed. He was keenly savoring its warmth and the delicious country smell of the mattress, which became even more pungent as it grew moist with his sweat. But at the same time he was in the whole house. Who knows if, at one moment in his dreams, he did not even become the house itself?

Throughout the night, he was conscious of the cows moving about in their stalls, and around four in the morning he heard the footsteps of a farm hand crossing the courtyard and the sound of the latch being lifted: what prevented him from actually seeing the man, by the light of a hurricane lamp, as he sat on a three-legged stool drawing the milk into tin buckets?

He must have fallen into a deep sleep again, for he woke up with a start at the sound of the toilet flushing. The sudden, violent noise gave him rather a fright. But immediately afterward he was back to his old tricks and imagined the master of the house coming out of the bathroom, with his suspenders around his thighs, and tiptoeing back to his room. Madame Naud was asleep, or pretending to be, with her face to the wall. Etienne Naud had left the room in darkness except for the small light above the dressing table. He started to shave, his fingers numbed by the icy water. His skin was pink, taut, and glossy.

Then he sat down in a chair to pull on his boots. Just as he was leaving the room, a sound came from beneath the blankets. What was his wife saying to him? He bent over her and murmured something in a low voice. He closed the door noiselessly behind him and tiptoed down the stairs. At this point, Maigret jumped out of bed and switched on the light. He had had enough of these spellbinding nocturnal activities.

He looked at his watch, which he had left on the bedside table. It was half past five. He listened carefully and decided that either it had stopped raining or the rain had turned into a fine, silent drizzle.

Admittedly, he had eaten and drunk well the previous evening, but he had not drunk too much. And yet this morning he felt as if he had drunk really heavily. As he took various things out of his suitcase he looked with heavy, swollen eyes at his unmade bed and in particular at that chair beside it.

He was convinced it had not been a dream: Geneviève Naud had come into his room. She had come in without knocking. She had positioned herself on that chair, sitting bolt upright without touching the back of it. At first, as he stared at her in sheer amazement, he had thought she was deranged. In reality, however, Maigret was infinitely more disturbed than she was. He had never been in such a delicate situation. Never before had a young girl who was ready to pour out her heart stationed herself at his bedside, with him in bed in his nightshirt, his hair ruffled by the pillow and his lips moist with spittle.

He had muttered something like:

"If you'll turn the other way for a moment, I'll get up and put some clothes on."

"It doesn't matter. . . . I have only a few words to say to you. . . . I am pregnant by Albert Retailleau. . . . If my father finds out, I'll kill myself; and no one will stop me."

He could not bring himself to look at her while he was lying in bed. She paused for a moment, as if expecting Maigret to react to her announcement, then rose to her feet, listened at the door, and said as she left the room:

"Do as you wish. I am in your hands."

Even now, he could scarcely believe all this had happened, and the thought that he had lain prostrate like a dummy throughout the proceedings humiliated him. He was not vain, in the way men can be, and yet he was ashamed that a young girl had caught him in bed with his face still bloated by sleep. And the girl's attitude was even more annoying; she had hardly glanced at him. She had not pleaded with him, as he might have expected, she had not thrown herself at his feet, she had not wept.

He recalled her face, its regular features making her look a little like her father. He could not have said if she was beautiful, but she had left him with an impression of maturity and poise, which even her insane overture had not dispelled.

"I am pregnant by Albert Retailleau. . . . If my father finds out, I'll kill myself; and no one will stop me."

Maigret finished dressing and mechanically lit his first pipe of the day. He then opened the door and, failing to find the light switch, groped his way along the hallway. He went down the stairs but could not see a light anywhere, even though he could hear someone stoking the stove. He made his way to where the noise was coming from and saw a shaft of yellow light beneath a door. He tapped gently, opened the door, and found himself in the kitchen.

Etienne Naud was sitting at one end of the table, his elbows resting on the light wood, and tucking into a bowl of soup. An elderly cook in a blue apron was sending showers of white-hot cinders into the ash bucket as she raked her stove.

Maigret saw the startled look on Naud's face as he came in and realized he was annoyed at having been caught unawares in the kitchen having his breakfast like a farm worker.

"Up already, Superintendent? I keep to the old country habits, you know. No matter what time I go to bed, I'm always up at five in the morning. I hope I didn't wake you?"

There was no point in telling him that it had been the sound of the toilet flushing that had awakened him.

"I won't offer you a bowl of soup, for I

presume you . . . ."

"But I'd love some."

"Léontine . . ."

"Yes, monsieur, I heard. . . . I'll have it ready in a moment."

"Did you sleep well?"

"Quite well. But at one point I thought I heard footsteps in the hallway. . . ."

Maigret had brought this up in order to find out whether Naud had pounced on his daughter after she had left his room, but the look of astonishment on his face seemed genuine enough.

"When? . . . I didn't hear anything. Though it's true it takes a lot to rouse me from my sleep early in the night. It was probably our friend Alban getting up to go to the bathroom. What do you think of him, incidentally? A likable fellow, isn't he? Far more cultured than he actually appears to be. He's read countless books, you know. . . . Pity he didn't have better luck with his wife."

"He was married, then?"

Having thought Groult-Cotelle to be the archetypal bachelor living in the provinces, Maigret viewed this snippet of information somewhat suspiciously. He felt as if they had hidden something from him, as if they

34

had deliberately tried to mislead him.

"Indeed he was, and, what's more, he still is. He has two children, a girl and a boy. The elder of the two must be twelve or thirteen now."

"Does his wife live with him?"

"No. She lives on the Côte d'Azur. It's rather a sad story, and no one ever talks about it around here. She came from a very good family, though. She was a Deharme. . . . Yes, like the General . . . She's his niece. A rather eccentric woman who could never grasp the fact that she was living in Saint-Aubin and not in Paris. She scandalized the neighborhood on several occasions, and then, one winter, moved to Nice, ostensibly to escape the bitter cold here, but of course she never came back. She lives there with her children. . . . And she's not living alone, needless to say."

"Didn't her husband ask for a divorce?"

"That's not done in these parts."

"Which of them has the money?"

Etienne Naud looked at him disapprovingly, and it was obvious he did not want to go into details.

"She is undoubtedly a very rich woman. . . ."

The cook had sat down at the table to grind the coffee in an old-fashioned coffee mill with a large copper top.

"You are lucky. It has stopped raining. But my brother-in-law really ought to have told you to bring some boots. After all, he comes from this part of the world and knows it well. We are right in the middle of the marshes and even have to use a boat in winter to reach some of my farms. They're known as *cabanes* here, by the way. . . . But speaking of my brother-in-law, I feel rather embarrassed he had the nerve to ask a man of your standing to . . ."

The question Maigret kept asking himself, the question that had been constantly on his mind ever since his arrival the previous evening, was: Were the Nauds decent people who had nothing to hide and who were doing their utmost to make their guest from Paris feel at home, or was he in fact an unwelcome intruder whom Bréjon had most inconsiderately deposited in their midst and whose presence this disconcerted couple could well have done without?

He decided to try an experiment.

"Not many people get off the train at Saint-Aubin," he commented as he ate his soup. "I think only two of us did yesterday, apart from an old peasant woman wearing a bonnet."

"Yes, you're right."

"Does the man who got off the train with me live around here?"

Etienne Naud hesitated before replying. Why? Maigret was looking at him so intently that he was covered with confusion.

"I'd never seen him before," he answered hurriedly. "You must have noticed me dithering as to which one of you to approach."

Maigret tried another tactic:

"I wonder what he has come here for, or, rather, who asked him to come."

"Do you know him?"

"He's a private detective. I'll have to find out where he is and what he is up to this morning. He presumably checked in at one or another of the inns you mentioned yesterday."

"I'll take you into town shortly in the pony cart."

"Thanks, but I'd rather walk, if you don't mind, and then I'll be free to come and go as I like."

Something had just occurred to him. Supposing Naud had been counting on him

37

to sleep soundly so that he could leave early for the village and meet Inspector Cavre?

Anything was possible here, and the Superintendent even began to wonder if the young girl's appearance in his room had not been part of a plot the whole family had planned.

A moment later, he dismissed such thoughts as foolish.

"I hope your daughter isn't seriously ill."

"No . . . Well, if you really want the truth, in spite of all we've done, she has got wind of what is being said around here. She's a proud young woman. All young women are. I'm sure that's the reason she has insisted on staying in her room for the past three days. And maybe your arrival has made her feel rather ashamed."

"Ashamed, is she!" thought Maigret, as he recalled her brief appearance in his room the night before.

"We can talk in front of Léontine," Naud went on. "She's known me from childhood. She's been with the family for . . . for how many years, Léontine?"

"Ever since I had my first communion, monsieur!"

"A little more soup? No? . . . To continue, I'm in a most awkward position, and I sometimes think my brother-in-law tackled the case in the wrong way. I'm sure you'll say he knows far more about such matters than I do; that's his job. . . . But maybe he has forgotten what it's like in our part of the world now that he lives in Paris."

It was hard to believe he was not speaking sincerely, since he seemed to want to talk over what was on his mind. He sat there with his legs apart, stuffing his pipe, while Maigret finished his breakfast. The kitchen smelled of the freshly made coffee, and the two men were enjoying the warm atmosphere of the room. Outside, in the darkness of the courtyard, the stable hand was whistling softly as he groomed one of the horses.

"To speak bluntly . . . From time to time, rumors about someone or other are spread around town. This time, it's a serious matter, I know. But I still wonder whether it would not be wiser to disregard the accusation. . . . You agreed to do what my brother-in-law asked. You have done us the honor of coming. . . . Everyone knows by now that you are here, that's for sure. Tongues are already wagging. No doubt you intend to question some people, and that is bound to stir their imaginations even more. . . . So that's why I really do wonder, quite sincerely, whether we are going about this whole business in the right way. . . . Are you sure you have had enough to eat? . . . If you don't mind the cold, I'll be glad to show you around. I go on a tour of inspection every morning."

Maigret was putting on his overcoat as the maid came downstairs; she got up an hour later than the old cook. The two men went out into the cold, damp courtyard and spent an hour going from one stable to another. Meanwhile, cans of milk were being loaded into a small truck.

Some cows were to be taken to market in a nearby town that very day and drovers in dark overalls were rounding them up. At the end of the yard was a small office with a little round stove, a table, ledgers, and a desk with an array of pigeonholes. Sitting at the table was a farm hand wearing the same sort of boots as his boss.

"Will you excuse me a moment?"

Madame Naud was getting up now, for there was a light on in her room on the second floor. The other rooms remained in darkness, which meant that Groult-Cotelle and the young girl were still fast asleep. The maid was cleaning the dining room.

Men and animals could be seen moving about in the dim light of the courtyard and outbuildings, and Maigret could hear the motor of the milk truck running in the background.

"That's done. . . . I was just giving a few instructions. . . . I'll be leaving by car for the market shortly; I've got to meet some other farmers. . . . If I had time, and thought you would be interested, I would tell you how the farm is run. I have ordinary dairy cattle on my other farms, since we supply the local dairy with milk, but here we breed only the finest, most of which we sell abroad. I even send some to South America. But right now, I am entirely at your service. . . . It will be daylight in an hour. If you need the car or if you have any questions you would like to ask me . . . I want you to feel comfortable. You must treat this as your home."

His face was cheerfully beaming as he spoke, but his smile faded when Maigret merely answered:

"Well, if you don't mind, I'll be on my way."

The road surface was spongy, as if water from the canal on the left had soaked the ground beneath. The railroad embankment ran along the right-hand side of the road. After a little more than half a mile, a glaring light became visible, obviously the one at the station, since green and red signals flashed nearby.

Maigret looked back toward the house and saw that there were lights on in two more windows on the second floor. This brought Alban Groult-Cotelle into his mind, and he began to wonder why he had been so put out to discover that he was married.

The sky was brightening. One of the first houses Maigret caught sight of as he turned to the left of the station and approached the village had a signboard reading LE LION D'OR. The lights were on downstairs, and he went inside. He found himself in a long, low room where everything was brown — the walls, the beams of the ceiling, the long polished tables, and the backless benches. A kitchen range at the very end of the room had not yet been lit. A woman of indeterminate age was crouched over a log burning slowly on the hearth, waiting for the coffee to heat. She turned around to look at the stranger, but said nothing. Maigret sat down in the dim light of a very dusty lamp.

"I'd like to sample the local brandy!" he said, shaking his overcoat, which the damp dawn had showered with grayish beads of moisture.

The woman did not reply, and he thought she had not heard. She went on stirring the saucepan of rather uninviting coffee with her spoon, and when it was to her liking she poured some into a cup, put it on a tray, and walked toward the staircase.

"I'll be down in a minute," she said.

Footsteps sounded above Maigret's head. He could hear voices but could not make out what was being said. Five minutes went by. Then another five. Every now and then Maigret rapped a coin on the wooden table, but nothing happened.

At last, a quarter of an hour later, the woman came downstairs again and spoke even less amicably than before.

"What did you say you wanted?"

"A glass of the local brandy."

"I haven't any."

"You've no brandy?"

"I've got cognac, but no local brandy."

"Then give me a cognac."

43

She gave him a glass so thick-bottomed that there was hardly any room for the drink.

"Tell me, madame . . . I believe a friend of mine arrived here last night."

"How am I to know if he's your friend?"

"Has he just got up?"

"I have one guest and I have just taken him his coffee."

"If he's the man I know, I bet he asked you lots of questions, didn't he?"

The glasses left by the previous evening's customers had made round wet marks on many of the tables, and the woman began to wipe them with a cloth.

"Albert Retailleau spent the evening here the day before he died, didn't he?"

"What's that got to do with you?"

"He was a good boy, I believe. Someone told me he played cards that evening. Is *belote* the favorite game in this part of the world?"

"No. We play *coinchée*."

"So he played *coinchée* with his friends. He lived with his mother, didn't he? A good woman, unless I'm mistaken."

"Hmm!"

"What's that?"

"Nothing. You're the one who's doing

all the talking, and I don't know what you're getting at."

Upstairs, Inspector Cavre was getting dressed.

"Does she live far from here?"

"At the end of the street, in a small yard. It's the house with three stone steps."

"Do you happen to know if my friend Cavre — the man who's staying here with you — has been to see her yet?"

"And just how do you think he could have been to see her when he's only just getting up?"

"Will he be staying long?"

"I haven't asked him."

She opened the windows and pushed back the shutters. A milky-white light filtered into the room, for day had come.

"Do *you* think Retailleau was drunk that night?"

The woman suddenly became aggressive and snapped back:

"No more drunk than you are, drinking cognac at eight in the morning!"

"How much do I owe you?"

"Two francs."

The Trois Mules, a rather more modern-looking inn, was right opposite, but the Superintendent did not think he would gain anything by going inside. A blacksmith was lighting the fire in his forge. A woman standing on her doorstep was throwing a bucket of dirty water into the street. A bell, the sound of which reminded Maigret of his childhood, tinkled lightly, and a boy wearing clogs came out of the baker's with a loaf of bread under his arm.

Curtains parted as he made his way down the street. A hand wiped the condensation from a window, and a wrinkled old face with eyes that were ringed with red like Inspector Cavre's peered through the windowpane. On the right stood the church. It was built of gray stone and roofed with slate, which looked black and shiny after the heavy rain. A very thin woman of about fifty, in deep mourning and holding herself very erect, came out of the church holding a missal bound in black cloth.

Maigret stood idly for a while in a corner of the little square next to a board marked SCHOOL, which had doubtless been put up to caution drivers. He followed the woman with his eyes. The minute he saw her disappear into a kind of blind alley at the end of the street, he guessed at once that it was Madame Retailleau. Since Cavre had not yet visited her, he quickened his step.

He had guessed right. When he got to the corner of the alley, he saw the woman go up three steps to the door of a small house and take a key out of her bag. A few minutes later, he knocked at the glass door, which was faced by a lace curtain.

"Come in."

She had just had time to take off her coat and her black crepe veil. The missal was still on the oilcloth-covered table. The white enamel kitchen stove was already lit. The top was so clean that it must have been painstakingly rubbed with fine sand-paper.

"Please forgive me for disturbing you, madame. Madame Retailleau, I presume?"

He wasn't very sure of himself, for neither her voice nor her gestures gave him much encouragement. She stood quite still, with her hands over her stomach, her face almost the color of wax, and waited for Maigret to speak.

"I have been asked to investigate the rumors that are circulating with regard to the death of your son."

"Who are you?"

"Superintendent Maigret of the Police Judiciaire. Let me hasten to add that these inquiries are for the moment unofficial."

"What does that mean?"

"That the case has not yet been brought before the court."

"What case?"

"I am sorry to have to talk about such unpleasant matters, madame, but you are no doubt aware of the various rumors connected with your son's death."

"You can't keep people from talking."

Stalling for time, Maigret turned toward a photograph in an oval frame that was hanging on the wall to the left of the walnut kitchen sideboard. It was an enlarged photograph of a man of about thirty with a crew cut and a large mustache drooping over his lips.

"Is that your husband?"

"Yes."

"Unless I'm misinformed, you had the misfortune to lose him unexpectedly when your son was still a small boy. From what I have been told, you were forced to bring an action against the dairy that employed him in order to receive a pension."

"You have been told nonsense. There was never any court case. Monsieur Oscar Drouhet, the manager of the dairy, did what was necessary."

"And later, when your son was old

enough to work, he gave him a job in the office. Your son was his bookkeeper, I believe."

"He did the work of an assistant manager. He would have been given the title if he hadn't been so young."

"You don't have a photograph of him, do you?"

Maigret could have kicked himself, for as he spoke he saw a tiny photograph on a small round table covered with red plush. He picked it up quickly, in case Madame Retailleau objected.

"How old was Albert when this photograph was taken?"

"Nineteen. It was taken last year."

A handsome boy, somewhat broad-faced, with sensuous lips and merry, sparkling eyes. He looked healthy and strong.

Madame Retailleau stood waiting, as before, heaving an occasional sigh.

"He wasn't engaged?"

"No."

"As far as you know, he had no relationships with women?"

"My son was too young to be chasing women. He was a serious boy and thought only about his career."

This was not the impression conveyed

49

by the lively look, the thick glossy hair, and the well-developed physique.

"What was your reaction when . . . I do apologize . . . You must see what I am getting at. . . . Do you believe it was an accident?"

"One has to believe it was."

"You had no suspicions whatsoever, then?"

"What sort of suspicions?"

"He never mentioned Mademoiselle Naud? . . . He never used to come home late at night?"

"No."

"And Monsieur Naud hasn't been to see you since your son's death?"

"We have nothing to say to each other."

"I see. . . . But he might have. . . . Monsieur Groult-Cotelle hasn't called on you either, I take it?"

Was it Maigret's imagination, or had her eyes hardened momentarily? Maigret was sure they had.

"No," she murmured.

"So you consider the rumors concerning the circumstances of your son's death to be quite unfounded?"

"Yes, I do. I pay no attention to them. I don't want to know what people are saying. And if it's Monsieur Naud who sent you, you can go back and tell him what I've said."

For a few seconds, Maigret stood perfectly still, with his eyes half-shut, and repeated to himself what she had said, as if to lodge it in his mind:

"And if it's Monsieur Naud who sent you, you can go back and tell him what I've said."

Did she know that it was Etienne Naud who had met Maigret at the station the day before? Did she know that it was he, indirectly, who had caused him to make the journey from Paris? Or did she merely suspect this to be the case?

"Forgive me for having taken the liberty of calling on you, madame, especially at such an early hour."

"Time is of no importance to me."

"Good-by, madame."

She remained where she was and said not a word as Maigret walked toward the door and closed it behind him. The Superintendent had not gone ten paces when he saw Inspector Cavre standing on the sidewalk as if he were on sentry duty.

Was Cavre waiting for Maigret to leave so that he, in turn, could talk to Albert's mother? Maigret wanted to make sure once

51

and for all. His conversation with Madame Retailleau had put him in a bad temper, and he was in the mood to play a trick on his former colleague.

He relit his pipe, which he had put out with his thumb before entering Madame Retailleau's house, crossed the street, and took up a position on the other side, immediately opposite Cavre, standing resolutely on the pavement as if he meant to stay.

The town was awakening. Children were walking up to the school gate on one side of the little square in front of the church. Most of them had come from far away and were muffled up in scarves and thick blue or red woolen socks. Many were wearing clogs.

"Well, Old Cadaver, it's your turn now! Your move!" Maigret seemed to be saying, with a mischievous glint in his eyes.

Cavre did not budge, but looked haughtily in the other direction, as if he were above such frivolities.

Had he been summoned to Saint-Aubin by Madame Retailleau? It was quite possible. She was a strange woman, and it was very difficult to size her up. She had a peasant streak, the characteristic, almost innate mistrust of the peasant; but there was also, in her make-up, more than a touch of the bourgeois upper crust of the provinces. Beneath the glacial exterior, one sensed an arrogance that nothing could undermine. The way she had faced Maigret, with stony immobility, was impressive in itself. She had not moved a step, or made any gesture, as long as he was in her house, but had frozen, as some animals are said to do when, up against danger, they simulate death. Her lips barely moved when she spoke.

"Well, Cavre, you old misery! Make up your mind. . . . Do something."

Old Cadaver was stamping his feet to keep warm but seemed in no hurry to make any sort of move as long as Maigret was watching him.

It was a ridiculous situation. It was childish to stay rooted where he was, but Maigret did just that. Unfortunately, however, this tactic turned out to be a waste of time. At half past eight, a small, red-faced man came out of his house and made his way to the town hall. He opened the door with a key, and a moment afterward Cavre followed him inside.

This was the very move that Maigret

had planned on making that morning. He had determined to find out what the local authorities had to say. His former colleague had beaten him to it, and he had no choice but to wait his turn.

—3—

An Undesirable Person

Maigret was to consider this undignified episode as unmentionable. He never spoke of what happened that day, and particularly that morning, and no doubt he would have preferred to forget all about it.

The most disconcerting experience was losing his sense of identity, of being Maigret. For what, in fact, did he represent in Saint-Aubin? Strictly speaking — nothing. Justin Cavre had gone into the town hall to talk to the local authorities while he, Maigret, had stood awkwardly outside in the street. The row of houses looked like a line of large, poisonous mushrooms, clustered as they were beneath a sky that reminded one of a blister ready to burst.

Maigret knew he was being watched; faces were peering at him from behind every curtain.

True, he did not really mind what a few old ladies or the butcher's wife thought of him. People were free to take him for what they liked and laugh at him as he went by, as some of the children passing through the school gate had done.

No, the trouble was that he did not feel in his proper skin — perhaps an exaggerated way of putting it, but there it is.

What would happen, for example, if he were to go into the whitewashed lobby of the town hall and knock at the gray door with SECRETARY'S OFFICE displayed in black letters? He would be asked to wait his turn, just as if he had come to ask for a birth certificate or about a claim of some sort. And meanwhile, Old Cadaver would continue questioning the secretary in his tiny overheated office for as long as he pleased.

Maigret was not here in an official capacity. He could not claim to be acting on behalf of the Police Judiciaire, and, anyway, who was to know whether anyone in this village surrounded by slimy marshes and stagnant water had even heard the name Maigret?

He was to find out soon enough. As he was waiting impatiently for Cavre to come out, he had one of the most extraordinary ideas of his entire career. He was all set to pursue his former colleague relentlessly, to follow him step by step and say, point-blank:

"Look here, Cavre, there's no point in trying to outwit each other. It is quite obvious you're not here for the fun of it. Someone asked you to come. Just tell me who it is and what you've been asked to do."

How comparatively simple a regular, official investigation seemed at this moment! Had he been on a case somewhere within his own jurisdiction he would only have had to go into the local post office and say:

"Superintendent Maigret. Get me the Police Judiciaire and make it snappy. . . . Hello! Is that you, Janvier? . . . Jump in your car and come down here. . . . When you see Old Cadaver come out . . . Yes, Justin Cavre . . . Right . . . Follow him and don't let him out of your sight."

Who knows? Maybe he would have had Etienne Naud tailed, too. He had just seen him drive past on the road to Fontenay.

Playing the role of Maigret was easy! An organization that ran like clockwork was at his disposal, and, what is more, he had only to say his name and people were so dazzled that they would go to any lengths to please him.

But here, he was so little known that despite the numerous articles and photographs that were always appearing in the newspapers, someone like Etienne Naud had walked straight up to Justin Cavre at the station.

Naud had welcomed Maigret effusively because his brother-in-law, the Examining Magistrate, had sent him all the way from Paris, but, on the other hand, had they not all behaved as if puzzled by his arrival? The gist of what their welcome meant was this:

"My brother-in-law, Bréjon, is a charming fellow, who wants to help, but he has been away from Saint-Aubin for too long and doesn't quite grasp the situation. It was kind of him to have thought of sending you here. It is kind of you to have come. We will look after you as best we can. Eat and drink your fill. Let me show you around the estate. But by no means feel constrained to stay in this damp, unattractive part of the world. And don't feel you have to look into this trivial matter, which concerns no one but ourselves."

On whose behalf was he working, anyway? For Etienne Naud. But it was palpably obvious that Etienne Naud did not want him to carry out a proper investigation.

And to cap it all, Geneviève had come into his room in the middle of the night and had admitted:

"I was Albert Retailleau's mistress and I am pregnant by him. But I'll kill myself if you breathe a word to my parents."

Now, if she really had been Albert's mistress, the accusations against Naud took on a terrible new meaning. Had she thought of that? Had she consciously charged her father with murder?

And even the victim's mother, who had said nothing, admitted nothing, denied nothing, in fact had made her meaning perfectly clear by her attitude:

"It's none of your business!"

Everyone, even the old ladies lying in wait behind their fluttering curtains, even the schoolchildren who had turned around to stare as they went by, considered him an intruder, an undesirable person. Worse still, no one knew where this steady plodder had come from or why he was in this village.

And so, in a setting just right, with hands deep in the pockets of his heavy overcoat, Maigret looked like one of those nasty characters tormented by some secret vice who prowl around the Porte Saint-Martin, or somewhere similar, with hunched shoulders and sidelong glances, and cautiously edge their way past the houses well out of sight of the police.

Was he turning into another Cavre? He felt like sending someone to Naud's house to get his suitcase and taking the first train back to Paris. He would tell Bréjon:

"They don't want me around there. . . . Leave your brother-in-law to his own devices."

And yet he had gone into the town hall as soon as the former inspector emerged, with a leather briefcase tucked under his arm. No doubt this would increase Cavre's standing in the village; now he would pass for a lawyer.

The secretary was a little man who smelled rather unpleasant. He did not get up when Maigret entered his office.

"Can I help you?"

"Superintendent Maigret of the Police Judiciaire. I am in Saint-Aubin on unofficial business and I would like to ask you one or two questions."

The little man hesitated and looked annoyed, but nonetheless bade Maigret sit down on a wicker chair.

"Did the private detective who has just left your office tell you whom he was working for?"

The secretary either did not understand or pretended he did not understand the question. And he reacted in similar fashion to all the other questions the Superintendent put to him.

"You knew Albert Retailleau. Tell me what you thought of him."

"He was a decent fellow. . . . Yes, that's how I'd describe him, a decent fellow. . . . Nothing to hold against him . . ."

"Was he a womanizer?"

"He was young, of course, and we don't always know what the young are up to, these days, but a womanizer . . . no, you couldn't call him that."

"Had he been Mademoiselle Naud's lover?"

"That's what people said. . . . Rumors

60

were going around. . . . But it's all pure hearsay."

"Who discovered the body?"

"Ferchaud, the stationmaster. He telephoned the town hall, and the Deputy Mayor immediately contacted the Benet Police Headquarters. There's no police sergeant in Saint-Aubin."

"What did the doctor who examined the body say?"

"What did he say? Just that he was dead . . . There wasn't much of him left. . . . The train went right over him."

"But he was identified as Albert Retailleau?"

"What? . . . Of course . . . It was Retailleau, all right; there was no doubt about that."

"When did the last train pass through?"

"At 5:07 in the morning."

"Didn't people think it odd that Retailleau was on the tracks at five in the morning in the middle of winter?"

The secretary's reply was curious:

"It was dry at the time. There was hoarfrost on the ground."

"But people talked just the same."

"Rumors circulated, yes. . . . But you

can never stop people from talking."

"Your opinion, then, is that Retailleau died a natural death?"

"It is very hard to say what happened."

And did Maigret bring up the subject of Madame Retailleau? He did, and the reply was as follows:

"She's an excellent woman. Nothing to be said against her."

And Naud, too, was described in similar terms:

"Such a pleasant man. His father was a splendid person, too, a county councillor."

And lastly, what did the secretary have to say about Geneviève?

"An attractive girl."

"Well behaved?"

"Of course she would be well behaved. . . . And her mother is one of the most respected members of the community."

All this was said politely enough, but without the ring of conviction, while the little man kept picking his nose and carefully examining what he had excavated.

"And what is your opinion of Monsieur Groult-Cotelle?"

"He's a decent fellow, too. Not stuck-up."

"Is he a close friend of the Nauds?"

"They see a good deal of one another, that's a fact. But that's only natural, since they move in the same circles."

"When exactly was Retailleau's cap discovered not far from the Nauds' house?"

"When? . . . Well . . . But was it just the cap that was found?"

"I was told that someone named Désiré who collects the milk for the dairy found the cap in the reeds along the bank of the canal."

"So people said."

"It's not true, then?"

"It's difficult to say. Désiré is drunk half the time."

"And when he is drunk . . ."

"Sometimes he tells the truth and sometimes he doesn't."

"But a cap is something you can see and touch! Some people have seen it."

"Ah!"

"It must have been put into safekeeping by now. . . ."

"Maybe . . . I don't know. . . . May I remind you that this office is not a police station, and we believe in minding our own business."

This unpleasant-smelling, seemingly half-witted individual could not have spoken more plainly, and was obviously delighted he had given a Parisian such short shrift.

A few moments later, Maigret was back in the street, no further on with his investigation, but by now convinced that no one was going to help him find the truth.

And since no one wanted to establish the truth, what was the point of his being here? Would it not be more sensible to go back to Paris and say to Bréjon:

"Look, your brother-in-law has no wish for a proper investigation. No one down there likes the idea. I have come back. They had a wonderful dinner for me."

Maigret passed a large house built of gray stone and saw from the bright-yellow plaque on the wall that it belonged to the notary. This, then, was the house that Bréjon's father and sister had once lived in, and in the watery gray light it had the same air of timelessness and inscrutability as the rest of the town.

He walked a little farther on, until he came to the Lion d'Or. Inside, he could see someone talking to the woman who ran the inn, and he had the distinct impression that they were talking about him and standing by the window in order to get a better view.

A man on a bicycle came into sight. Maigret recognized the rider as he approached but did not have time to turn away. Alban Groult-Cotelle was on his way home from the Nauds' and he jumped off his bicycle as soon as he saw Maigret.

"It's good to see you again. . . . We're only a stone's throw from my house. Will you do me the honor of coming in for a drink? . . . I insist. . . . My house is very modest but I've got a few bottles of vintage port."

Maigret followed him. He did not expect much to come of the visit but the prospect was vastly preferable to wandering alone through the hostile town.

It was a huge, solid house, which looked very appealing from a distance. Its squat shape, black ironwork, and high slate roof gave it the air of a bourgeois fortress.

Inside, everything was shabby and neglected. The surly-faced maid looked really slovenly, and yet it was obvious to Maigret, from certain looks they exchanged, that Groult-Cotelle was sleeping with her.

"I am sorry everything is so untidy. . . . I'm a bachelor and live alone. . . . I'm only interested in books, so . . ."

So . . . the wallpaper was peeling off the walls, which were covered with damp patches, the curtains were gray with dust, and one had to try three or four chairs before finding one that did not wobble. Only one room on the ground floor was heated, no doubt to save wood, and this served as a living room, dining room, and library. There was even a couch in one corner, which Maigret suspected his host slept on most of the time.

"Do sit down. . . . It really is a pity you didn't come in the summer, since it is rather more attractive around here then. . . . How do you like my friends the Nauds? . . . What a nice family they are! I know them well. You would not find a better man than Naud anywhere. He may not be a very deep thinker, he may be a tiny bit arrogant, but he is so unaffected and sincere. . . . He is very rich, you know."

"And Geneviève Naud?"

"A charming girl . . . without any . . . yes, charming is how I'd describe her."

"I presume I'll have the opportunity to meet her. . . . She'll soon be better, I hope?"

"Of course she will . . . of course. . . .
You know what girls her age are like. . . .
Cheers!"

"Did you know Retailleau?"

"By sight . . . His mother seems to be
well thought of. . . . I would show you
around if you were staying longer; there
are some interesting people here and there
in the villages. . . . My uncle the General used to say that it is in country dis-
tricts, and especially here in our Vendée,
that . . ."

Hot air! If Maigret gave Groult-Cotelle
the chance, he would start retelling him
the history of every family in the neighborhood.

"I am afraid I must go now."

"Oh, yes! Your investigation. . . . How
are you getting on? Are you optimistic?
. . . If you want my opinion, the answer
is to get hold of whoever is responsible for
all these false rumors."

"Have you any idea who it might be?"

"Me? Of course not. Don't start thinking
I have any bright ideas on the subject,
please. . . . I'll probably see you this
evening. Etienne has asked me to dinner,
and unless I'm too busy . . ."

Busy doing what, good God! Words in

this particular part of the world took on a completely different meaning.

"Have you heard the rumor about the cap?"

"What cap? Oh, yes . . . I was lost for a moment. . . . I did hear some vague story. . . . But is it true? Has it really been found? That's the key to it all, isn't it?"

No, that was not the key to it all. The young girl's confession, for example, was just as important as the discovery of the cap. But would Maigret be able to keep what he knew to himself much longer?

Five minutes later, Maigret rang the doctor's bell. A maid of sorts answered the door and started to explain that the office was closed until one o'clock. He persisted, and was shown into the garage, where a tall, strapping man with a cheerful face was repairing a motorcycle.

It was the same story:

"Superintendent Maigret of the Police Judiciaire . . . I'm here in an unofficial capacity. . . ."

"I'll show you into my office, if I may, and then when I've washed my hands . . ."

Maigret waited near the hinged, oilcloth-covered table that was used for examining patients.

"So you're the famous Superintendent Maigret? I've heard quite a lot about you. . . . I've a friend who pores over the miscellaneous news items in the papers. He lives more than twenty miles away, but if he knew you were in Saint-Aubin, he'd be over here in a flash. . . . You solved the Landru case, didn't you?"

He had hit on one of the few cases Maigret had had nothing to do with.

"And to what do we owe the honor of your presence in Saint-Aubin? For it is, indeed, an honor. . . . I am sure you would like a drink. . . . I have a sick child in the living room at the moment — it's warmer there — so I had to bring you in here. . . . Will you have a brandy?"

And that was it. All Maigret garnered from his visit was a brandy.

"Retailleau? A charming boy . . . I believe he was a good son to his mother. . . . Anyway, she never complained about him. She's one of my patients . . . a curious woman, whom life ought to have treated better. She came from a good family, too. Everyone was amazed when she married Joseph Retailleau, a workman at the dairy.

"Etienne Naud? He's a real character. . . . We go shooting together. He's a crack shot. . . . Groult-Cotelle? No, you could hardly call him a good shot, but that's because he is very near-sighted. . . .

"So, you have met everyone already. . . . Have you seen Clémentine, too? . . . You haven't seen Tine yet? . . . Note that I mention her name with great respect, like everyone else in Saint-Aubin. Tine is Madame Naud's mother . . . Madame Bréjon, if you prefer. . . . Her son is an examining magistrate in Paris. . . . Yes, that's right . . . he's the one you know, of course. His mother was a La Noue, one of the great families in the Vendée. She does not want to be a burden to her daughter and son-in-law and she lives by herself, near the church. . . . At the age of eighty-two, she's still sound of wind and limb and she's one of my worst patients.

"You're staying in Saint-Aubin for a few days, are you? . . .

"What? The cap? Oh, yes . . . No, I haven't heard anything about that my- self. . . . Well, I did hear one or two rumors. . . .

"All this was discovered rather late in the day, you see. . . . If I had known at the time, I would have done an autopsy.

But put yourself in my position. I was told the poor boy had been run over by a train. It was patently obvious to me he *had* been run over by a train, and naturally I wrote my report along those lines."

Maigret scowled. He could have sworn that they were all in league with one another, that whether peevish or merry like the doctor, they had passed around the story as they might pass around a ball, exchanging knowing looks as they did so.

The sky was almost bright now. Reflections shone in all the puddles, and patches of mud glistened in places.

The Superintendent walked up the main street once more. He had not looked to see what it was called but it was most probably Rue de la République. He decided to go into the Trois Mules, opposite the Lion d'Or, where he had received such a cold welcome that morning.

The bar was brighter than that of the Lion d'Or. There were framed prints and a photograph of a president who had held office some thirty or forty years earlier hanging on the whitewashed walls. Behind the bar was another room, deserted and gloomy-looking; this was evidently where the local people came to dance on Sundays,

71

for there was a platform at one end and the room was festooned with paper chains.

Four men were seated at a table, enjoying a bottle of full-bodied wine. One of them coughed affectedly when the Superintendent came in, as if to say to the others:

"There he is."

Maigret sat down on one of the benches at the other end of the room. He felt the atmosphere had changed. The men had stopped talking, and he knew full well that, before he came in, they would certainly not have been sitting there drinking and looking at each other in dead silence.

They looked just like characters in a dumb show as they sat in a huddle, elbows and shoulders touching. Eventually, the oldest of the four, a plowman, by the look of the whip beside him, spat on the floor, whereupon the others burst out laughing.

Was that long stream of spittle meant for Maigret?

"What will you have?" inquired a young woman, tilting her hips in order to support her grubby-looking baby.

"I'd like some of your *vin rosé*."

"A carafe?"

"All right."

Maigret puffed furiously at his pipe. Up till now the townsfolk had concealed, or at any rate disguised, their hostility toward him, but now they were openly sneering at him — indeed, deliberately provoking him.

"Even the dirtiest jobs need to be done, if you ask me, sonny boy," said the plowman after a long silence, although no one had asked him for his opinion in the first place.

His cronies roared with laughter, as if that simple pronouncement had some extraordinary significance for them. One man, however, did not laugh, a youth of eighteen or nineteen with pale-gray eyes and a spotty face. Leaning on one elbow, he looked Maigret straight in the eye, as if he wanted him to feel the force of his hatred or contempt.

"Some people have no pride!" growled another man.

"If you've got the cash, pride doesn't often come into it."

Perhaps their remarks did not amount to anything much, but Maigret got the message, nonetheless. He had finally clashed with the opposition party, to describe the situation in political terms.

Who could know for sure? Undoubtedly, all the rumors flying about had originated in the Trois Mules. And if the townspeople laid the blame at Maigret's door, they obviously thought Etienne Naud was paying him to hush up the truth.

"Tell me, gentlemen . . ."

Maigret rose to his feet and walked toward them. Although not timid by nature, he felt the blood rushing to his ears.

He was greeted by total silence. Only the young man went on glowering at the Superintendent, while the others, looking rather awkward, turned their heads away.

"Those of you who live around here may be able to help me, in the interest of justice."

They were suspicious. Maigret's words had certainly stirred them up, but they still would not give in. The old man muttered crossly, looking at his spittle on the floor:

"Justice for who? For Naud?"

The Superintendent ignored the remark and went on talking. Meanwhile, the proprietress hovered in the kitchen doorway with the child in her arms.

"For justice to prevail, I need to discover two things in particular. First, I need to find one of Retailleau's friends, a real friend and, if possible, someone who was with him on that last evening. . . ."

Maigret realized that the person in question was the youngest of the four men, for the other three glanced in his direction.

"Secondly, I need to find the cap. You know what I'm talking about."

"Speak up, Louis!" growled the plowman, as he rolled a cigarette.

But the young man was not convinced.

"Who are you working for?"

It was certainly the first time Maigret's authority had been questioned by a country boy. And yet it was essential that he explain himself, since he was determined to gain the young man's confidence.

"Superintendent Maigret, Police Judiciaire."

Who knows? Perhaps luck would have it that the young man had heard of him. But alas, this was not the case.

"Why are you staying with the Nauds?"

"Because he was told I was coming and was at the station to meet me. And, since I didn't know the neighborhood . . ."

"There are inns."

"I didn't know that when I arrived."

"Who's the man in the inn across the road?"

It was Maigret who was being interrogated!

"A private detective."

"Who's he working for?"

"I don't know."

"Why has there still been no proper investigation into what happened? Albert died three weeks ago."

"That's the way, boy! Go on!" the three men seemed to be saying as the young man stood rigidly in front of them with a grim look on his face in an effort to combat his shyness.

"No one registered a complaint."

"So you can kill anyone, and so long as no one registers a complaint . . ."

"The doctor concluded that it was an accident."

"Was he there when it happened?"

"As soon as I have enough evidence, the investigation will be made official."

"What do you mean by evidence?"

"Well, if we could prove that the cap was discovered between Naud's house and the place where the body was found, for example . . ."

"We'll have to take him to Désiré," said

the stoutest of the men, who was wearing a carpenter's coverall. "Another round, Mélie . . . and one more glass."

For Maigret, it was a victory.

"What time did Retailleau leave the café that night?"

"About half past eleven."

"Were there many people in the café?"

"Four . . . We played *coinchée*."

"Did you all leave together?"

"The two other men took the road to the left. . . . I went part of the way with Albert."

"In which direction?"

"Toward Naud's house."

"Did Albert confide in you?"

"No."

The young man's face darkened. He said no reluctantly, since he obviously wanted to be scrupulously honest.

"He didn't say why he was going to the Nauds'?"

"No. He was very angry."

"Who with?"

"With her."

"You mean Mademoiselle Naud? Had he told you about her before?"

"Yes."

"What did he tell you?"

"Everything and nothing . . . Not in words . . . He used to go there nearly every night."

"Did he brag about it?"

"No." He gave Maigret a reproachful look. "He was in love; everyone could see that. He couldn't hide it."

"And he was angry with her on that last day?"

"Yes. Something was on his mind the whole evening. He kept looking at his watch as we played cards. Just as we parted on the road . . ."

"Where exactly?"

"Five hundred yards from the Nauds' house."

"The place, then, where he was found dead?"

"More or less . . . I had gone halfway with him. . . ."

"And you are sure he went on along the road?"

"Yes . . . He squeezed my hands and said, with tears in his eyes:

" 'It's all over, Louis.' "

"What was all over?"

"It was all over between him and Geneviève. . . . That's what I assumed. . . . He meant he was going to

78

see her for the last time."

"But did he go?"

"There was a moon that night. . . . It was freezing. . . . I could still see him when he was only about a hundred yards from the house."

"And the cap?"

Young Louis got up and looked at the others, his mind made up.

"Come with me. . . ."

"Can you trust him, Louis?" asked one of the older men. "Watch out, son."

But Louis was at the age when one is prepared to risk all to win all. He looked Maigret in the eye, as if to say:

"You're a real bastard if you let me down!"

"Come along . . . it's just a few steps."

"Your glass, Louis, and yours, Superintendent . . . And you can believe everything the boy says, I promise. . . . He's as honest as they come, that boy. . . ."

"Your good health, gentlemen."

Maigret had no choice but to drink a toast with the four men. The large glasses made a tinkling sound as they clinked them together. He then followed Louis out of the room, completely forgetting to pay for this carafe of wine.

As they came out, Maigret saw Old Cadaver on the opposite side of the street. He had his briefcase under his arm and was about to go into the Lion d'Or. Was Maigret mistaken? It seemed to him that his former colleague was smiling sardonically, although all he could see was the side of his face.

"Come with me. . . . This way."

They went along narrow lanes that Maigret hadn't even guessed existed and that linked the three or four streets in the village.

They came to a row of cottages, each with its own tiny fenced-in front garden. Louis pushed open a small gate with a bell attached to it and called out:

"It's me!"

He went into a kitchen, where four or five children were sitting around a table having their lunch.

"What is it, Louis?" asked his mother, looking uncomfortably at Maigret.

"Wait here. . . . I'll be back in a minute, monsieur."

Louis rushed up the stairs, which led straight out of the kitchen, and went into a room. Maigret heard the sounds of a drawer being pulled open, of quick steps and a chair knocked over. Meanwhile, Louis's mother did not quite know whether to make Maigret welcome or not, but at least she shut the kitchen door.

Louis came downstairs pale and worried-looking.

"Someone's stolen it!" he declared, stony-faced.

And then, turning to his mother, he said in a harsh voice:

"Someone's been here. . . . Who was it? Who came here this morning?"

"Look, Louis . . ."

"Who? Tell me who it was! Who stole the cap?"

"I don't even know what cap you're talking about."

"Someone went up to my room."

He was in such a state of excitement that he looked as if he would hit his mother.

"Will you please calm down! Can't you hear yourself speaking in that rude tone of voice?"

"Have you been in the house all morning?"

"I went out to the butcher's and the baker's. . . ."

"And what about the children?"

"I took the two boys next door, as

usual." She meant the two who were not yet of school age.

"Forgive me, Superintendent. I just don't understand. The cap was in my drawer this morning. I am positive it was. I saw it."

"But what cap are you talking about? Will you answer me? You're behaving as though you've gone out of your mind! Why don't you sit down and have something to eat? And this gentleman you've left standing . . ."

Louis gave his mother a pointed look, full of suspicion, and pulled Maigret outside.

"Come . . . there's something else I have to tell you. I swear, on my father's dead body, that the cap . . ."

—4—

The Theft of the Cap

The impatient young man walked quickly up the lane, his neck taut and his body bent forward as he pulled the massive

Maigret along with him. The Superintendent continued to be embarrassed by the
awkwardness of his situation. What did
they look like, the pair of them? The
younger, talking volubly, dragging the older
man along, not unlike the young hustlers
in Montmartre trying to propel some
intimidated provincial, almost against his
will, toward dubious delights.

Louis's mother stood on the doorstep,
and as they were turning the corner, she
shouted:

"Aren't you going to have something to
eat, Louis?"

Was he even listening? He was possessed
by violent emotion. He had promised
something to this gentleman from Paris
and now was unable to keep his word
because an unforeseen event had occurred.
Would he not be taken for an impostor?
Was he not endangering the cause he had
all too hastily championed?

"I want Désiré to tell you himself. The
cap was in my bedroom. I wonder if my
mother was telling the truth."

Maigret was wondering the same thing
and at the same time thought of Inspector
Cavre, whom he could picture vividly
wheedling information out of the woman

surrounded by children.

"What time is it?"

"Ten after twelve."

"Désiré will still be at the dairy. Let's go this way. It's quicker."

Louis led Maigret through alleyways and past small, shabby houses which came as a surprise to the Superintendent. Once, a mud-covered sow rushed at their legs.

"One night — the night of the funeral, in fact — old Désiré came into the Lion d'Or and threw a cap on the table, asking whether anyone knew whose it was. I recognized it at once, because I was with Albert when he bought it in Niort. I remember our discussing which color he should choose.

"What is your job?" asked Maigret.

"I'm a carpenter. The largest of the men you saw just now in the Trois Mules is my boss. Well, Désiré was drunk that night. There were at least six people in the café. I asked him where he had found the cap. Désiré collects the milk from the small farms in the marshes, you see, and since you can't get to them by road in a truck, he does his rounds by boat. . . .

" 'I found it in the reeds,' he said, 'close to the dead poplar.'

"There were at least six people who heard him say this. Everyone here knows that the dead poplar is between the Nauds' house and the spot where Albert's body was found. . . .

"This way . . . We're going to the dairy. You can see the chimney over there, on the left."

The village was now behind them. Dark hedges enclosed tiny gardens. A little farther on, the dairy came into view. The low buildings were painted white, and the tall chimney stood straight up against the sky.

"I don't know why I decided to shove the cap into my pocket. . . . I already had the feeling that too many people were eager to hush up the whole thing. . . .

" 'It's young Retailleau's cap,' someone said.

"And Désiré, drunk as he was, frowned. He suddenly realized that he was not supposed to have found it where he did.

" 'Désiré, are you sure it was near the dead poplar?'

" 'Why shouldn't I be sure?'

"Well, Superintendent, the very next day, he didn't want to admit to anything. When he was asked where exactly he had found the cap, he answered:

" 'Over there . . . I don't really know exactly. Just leave me alone, will you! I'm sick of this cap business. . . .' "

Flat-bottomed boats filled with milk cans were tied up beside the dairy.

"Hello, Philippe. Has old Désiré gone home?"

"He can't have gone home, because he never left home. . . . He must have got plastered yesterday — he didn't do his round this morning."

An idea flashed into Maigret's mind.

"Would the manager be around at this time of day, do you think?" he asked his companion.

"He'll probably be in his office. . . . The little door at the side."

"Wait here a minute."

Oscar Drouhet, the manager of the dairy, was on the telephone when Maigret walked in. The Superintendent introduced himself. Drouhet had the gravity and poise of the local craftsman turned small businessman. Pulling on his pipe with short, sharp puffs, he watched Maigret and let him speak, trying to size him up.

"Albert Retailleau's father once worked for you, I believe? I've been told he was killed in an accident at the dairy."

"One of the boilers exploded."

"I understand his widow receives a sizable compensation from you?"

He was an intelligent man and he realized immediately that Maigret's question was loaded with innuendos.

"What do you mean?"

"Did his widow take you to court, or did you yourself . . ."

"Don't try to complicate the issue. It was my fault that the accident happened. Retailleau had been saying for at least two months that the boiler needed a complete overhaul, and even that it should be replaced. It was the busiest time of the year, and I kept putting it off."

"Were your workmen insured?"

"Nowhere near adequately . . ."

"Excuse me. Let me ask you whether you were the one who thought they were inadequately insured, or if . . ."

Once more, they both understood each other perfectly, and Maigret did not have to finish his sentence.

"His widow registered a complaint against us, as she was entitled to do," Oscar Drouhet admitted.

"I am sure," the Superintendent went

on, smiling slightly, "that she did not simply come to ask you to consider the question of compensation pay. She sent lawyers to investigate. . . ."

"Is that so unusual? Women are ignorant in such matters, you'll agree. I acknowledged the validity of her claim, and in addition to the pension she received from the insurance company, I decided to give her a supplementary sum, which I pay out of my own pocket. On top of this, I paid for her son's education and gave him a job as soon as he was old enough to work. My kindness was rewarded, what's more, since he was a hard-working, honest fellow. Albert was clever and quite capable of running the dairy in my absence."

"Thank you . . . or, rather, just one more question: Albert's mother hasn't called on you since the death of her son, has she?"

Drouhet managed not to smile, but his brown eyes flickered briefly.

"No," he said, "she hasn't come to see me *yet*."

Maigret had been right, then, in this respect. Madame Retailleau was indeed a woman who knew how to defend herself, and to attack, if need be. She was undoubtedly the sort of person who would never lose sight of her interests.

"It seems that Désiré, your milk collector, did not come to work this morning?"

"That's not exceptional. . . . On the days when he is more drunk than usual . . ."

Maigret went back to the spotty youth, who was terrified he would no longer be taken seriously.

"What did he say? He's a decent man, but he's really on the other side."

"Whose side?"

"Monsieur Naud's, the doctor's, the Mayor's . . . He couldn't have said anything against me."

"Of course not . . ."

"We've got to find old Désiré. . . . We could go around to his house, if you like. . . . It's not very far."

They set off again, both forgetting it was lunchtime, and eventually came to a house on the fringe of the little town. Louis knocked on a door with a window in it, pushed it open, and shouted into the semidarkness:

"Désiré! Hey! Désiré!"

But only a cat emerged, and rubbed itself against the young man's legs. Meanwhile, Maigret came upon a kind of den, which contained a bed without a cover or pillow, where Désiré obviously slept with all his clothes on, a small, cracked iron stove, a bundle of rags, empty bottles, and gnawed bones.

"He must have gone off drinking somewhere. Come on. . . ."

Still the same concern that he would not be taken seriously.

"He worked on Etienne Naud's farm, you see. . . . He's still on good terms with them, even though he was fired. He's the sort of person who wants to be on good terms with everyone, and that's why he put on an act when people started asking him questions about the cap the day after he found it.

" 'What cap? Ah, yes! The tattered one I picked up someplace or other; I don't know where. . . . I've no idea what's happened to it.'

"Well, monsieur, I, for one, can tell you that there were bloodstains on the cap. And I wrote and told the Public Prosecutor. . . ."

"So it was you who wrote the anonymous letters?"

"I wrote three. If there were more,

someone else must have written them. I wrote about the cap and then about Albert's relationship with Geneviève Naud. . . . Wait, perhaps Désiré is in here."

Louis darted into a grocer's shop. Through the windows Maigret could see bottles at the end of the counter and two tables at the back of the shop for the use of customers. The young man looked crestfallen when he came out.

"He was here early this morning. He must have done the rounds."

Maigret had only been into two cafés: the Lion d'Or and the Trois Mules. In less than half an hour, he came to know a dozen or more, not cafés in the true sense of the word, but premises the average passer-by would not have suspected were licensed. The harness maker had a kind of bar next to his workshop, and the farrier had a similar arrangement. Old Désiré had been seen in almost every bar they visited.

"How was he?"

"He was all right enough."

And they knew what that meant.

"He was in a hurry when he left. He had to go to the post office."

"The post office is closed," Louis said. "But I know the postmistress, and she'll open up if I tap on her window."

"Especially when she learns I have a call to make," said Maigret.

And, sure enough, as soon as the boy tapped on the pane, the window opened.

"Is that you, Louis? What do you want?"

"The gentleman from Paris wants to make a call."

"I'll open up right away."

Maigret asked to be put through to the Nauds.

"Hello! Who is speaking?"

He did not recognize the voice, a man's voice.

"Hello! Who did you say? . . . Ah! Forgive me . . . Alban, yes . . . I hadn't realized. . . . This is Maigret. . . . Could you tell Madame Naud I won't be back for lunch? Give her my apologies. No, it's nothing important. . . . I don't know when I'll be back. . . ."

As he left the booth, he saw from the look on his young companion's face that he had something interesting to tell him.

"How much, mademoiselle? . . . Thank you . . . I'm sorry to have bothered you."

Back in the street once more, Louis informed Maigret excitedly:

"I *told* you something was up. Old Désiré came in on the dot of eleven. Do you know what he mailed? He sent a money order for five hundred francs to his son in Morocco. . . . His son's a good-for-nothing. He left home without any warning. He and his father used to quarrel and fight every day. . . . Désiré's never been known to be anything but drunk, you might say. . . . And now his son writes to him from time to time, either complaining or asking for money. . . . But all his money goes on drink, you see. . . . The old man never has a sou. . . . Sometimes he sends a money order for ten or twenty francs at the beginning of the month. . . . I wonder . . . Wait a minute. . . . If you still have time, we'll go and see his stepsister."

The streets, the houses they had been walking past all morning were now becoming familiar to the Superintendent. He was beginning to recognize people's faces and the names painted above the shops. Rather than brightening up, the sky had clouded over again and the air was heavy with moisture. Soon there would be fog.

"His stepsister knits for a living. She's an old spinster and used to work for our former priest. This is her house."

He went up the three steps to the blue-painted front door, knocked, and then opened it.

"Désiré's not here, is he?"

He then beckoned Maigret to come inside.

"Hello, Désiré . . . I'm sorry to barge in like this, Mademoiselle Jeanne. . . . There's a gentleman from Paris who'd like to have a few words with your stepbrother."

The tiny room was spotless. The table stood near a mahogany bed covered with an enormous red eiderdown. Maigret glanced around and saw a crucifix with a sprig of boxwood behind it, a figure of the Virgin Mary in a glass case on the chest of drawers, and two cutlets on a plate with a decorated border.

Désiré tried to stand up but knew he was in danger of falling off his chair. He maintained a dignified pose and, muttering thickly, his tongue unable to articulate the words, brought out:

"What can I do for you?"

For he was polite. He was always anxious to make that clear.

"I may have been drinking too much. . . . Yes, maybe I've had more than one drink, but I *am* polite, mon-

94

sieur. . . . Everyone'll tell you that Désiré is polite to one and all."

"Look, Désiré, the gentleman wants to know exactly where you found the cap. . . . You know, Albert's cap."

These few words were enough. The drunkard's face hardened and assumed a totally blank expression. His watery eyes became even more glaucous.

"Don't know what you mean."

"Don't be a fool, Désiré. . . . I've got the cap. . . . You remember when you threw it on the table at François's place, that evening, and said you'd found it by the dead poplar. . . ."

The old monkey was not satisfied with a simple denial. He smirked with delight and went on with more gusto than was necessary:

"Do you understand what he's saying, m'sieur? Why should I have thrown a cap on the table, I'd like to know? I've never worn a cap. . . . Jeanne! Where's my hat? Show this gentleman my hat. . . . These youngsters have no respect for their elders."

"Désiré . . ."

"Désiré, indeed! . . . Désiré may be drunk, but he's polite and would be obliged if you'd call him Monsieur Désiré. . . ."

95

Do you hear, you snotnose, you fatherless bastard!"

"Have you heard from your son recently?" Maigret interrupted suddenly.

"So, it's my son, now, eh? You want to know what my son's been up to? Well, just let me tell you. He's a soldier! He's a brave fellow, my son!"

"That's what I thought. He'll certainly be pleased with the money order."

"Soon I won't be allowed to send my son a money order, is that it? Hey, Jeanne! Do you hear? And maybe I won't be allowed to come and have a bite to eat with my stepsister either!"

At first, he had probably been frightened, but now he was really enjoying himself. He played the fool for his own entertainment, and when Maigret got up to go, he followed him out to the front doorstep, staggering all the way, and would have followed him into the street if Jeanne had not stopped him.

"Désiré's polite. . . . Do you hear, you rascal? And if anyone tells you, Monsieur le Parisien, that Désiré's son is not a fine, upstanding fellow . . ."

Doors opened. Maigret was glad to get away.

With tears in his eyes and clenched teeth, Louis stuttered:

"I swear to you, Superintendent . . ."

"It's all right, my boy. I believe you. . . ."

"It's that man staying at the Lion d'Or, isn't it?"

"I think so. I'd like to have proof, though. Do you know anyone who was at the Lion d'Or last night?"

"I'm sure Liboureau's son was there. He goes there every evening."

"I'll wait at the Trois Mules while you go and ask him if he saw Désiré. Find out if the old man got into conversation with our visitor from Paris. . . . Wait a minute. . . . We can eat at the Trois Mules, can't we? We'll have a bite of something together. . . . Off you go. Be quick!"

There was no tablecloth. The table was set with steel knives and forks. All that was offered at noon was a beet salad, a rabbit stew, and a piece of cheese, with some poor white wine. When Louis returned, however, he felt very uncomfortable sitting at the Superintendent's table.

"Well?"

"Désiré went to the Lion d'Or."

"Did he talk to Old Cadaver?"

"To who?"

"Never mind. It's a nickname we gave him. Did Désiré talk to him?"

"It didn't happen like that. The man you call Cadav . . . It sounds really odd to me. . . ."

"His name is Justin Cavre."

"Monsieur Cavre, according to Liboureau, spent a good part of the evening watching the cardplayers and saying nothing. Désiré was drinking in his usual corner. He left at about ten o'clock, and a few minutes later Liboureau noticed that the Parisian had disappeared, too. But he doesn't know if he left the inn or just went upstairs."

"He left."

"What are you going to do?"

He was so proud to be working with the Superintendent that he could not wait to get started.

"Who was it who reported seeing a considerable sum of money in Madame Retailleau's house?"

"The postman, Josaphat . . . Another alcoholic . . . He's called Josaphat because when his wife died he had more to drink than usual and kept on saying through his tears:

" 'Good-by, Céline . . . We'll meet again in the valley of Josaphat. . . . Count on me. . . .' "

"What would you like for dessert?" asked the proprietress, who obviously had one of her children on her arm all day and worked with her one free hand. "I've cookies or apples."

"Make your choice," said Maigret.

And the young man replied, blushing:

"I don't care. . . . Some cookies, please . . . This is what happened. . . . About ten or twelve days after Albert's funeral, the postman went to collect for a delivery from Madame Retailleau. She was busy doing the housework. She looked in her purse but she needed fifty francs more. So she walked over to the sideboard, where the soup tureen is. . . . You must have noticed it. It's got blue flowers on it. . . . She stood in front of it so that Josaphat couldn't see what she was doing, but that evening he swore he had seen some thousand-franc notes — at least ten, he said, maybe more. . . . Now, everybody knows that Madame Retailleau has never had that much money at one time. . . . Albert spent all he earned."

"What did he spend it for?"

"He was rather vain. . . . There's nothing wrong with that. He liked to be well dressed and he had his suits made in Niort. . . . He would often pay for a round of drinks, too. . . . He would tell his mother that as long as she had her pension . . ."

"They quarreled, then?"

"Sometimes . . . Albert was an independent fellow, you see. . . . His mother wanted to treat him like a little boy. If he had listened to her, he would have stayed home at night and he'd never have set foot in the café. . . . My mother's just the opposite. She can't get me out of the house quick enough."

"Where can we find Josaphat?"

"He'll probably be at home now, or else about to finish his first round. In half an hour he'll be at the station to collect the bags with the second mail. . . ."

"Will you bring us some liqueur, please, madame?"

Maigret stared through the curtains at the windows on the other side of the street, imagined Old Cadaver eating his lunch, the same as he was, and watching him the same way. It was not long before he realized his mistake. A car came noisily to a halt opposite the Lion d'Or, and Cavre got out, his briefcase under his arm. Maigret watched him lean over toward the driver to find out how much he owed.

"Whose car is that?"

"It belongs to the man who owns the garage. We went past it a little while ago. He acts as a taxi driver occasionally, if someone's ill and needs to be taken to the hospital, or if there's some other emergency."

The car made a half-turn and, judging from the noise, obviously did not go far.

"You see. He's gone back to his garage."

"Are you on good terms with him?"

"He's a friend of my boss."

"Go and ask him where he took his client this morning."

Less than five minutes later, Louis came running back.

"He went to Fontenay-le-Comte. It's exactly thirteen miles from here."

"Didn't you ask him where they went in Fontenay?"

"He was told to stop at the Café du Commerce, on Rue de la République. The man from Paris went in, came out with another man, and told the driver to wait."

"You don't know who this man was?"

"The garage man didn't know him. . . . They were gone about half an hour. Then the man you call Cavre was driven back. He only gave a five-franc tip."

Hadn't Etienne Naud also gone to Fontenay?

"Let's go and see Josaphat."

He had already left his house. They met up with him at the station, where he was waiting for the train. When he saw young Louis with Maigret, from the other end of the platform, he looked annoyed and went hurriedly into the stationmaster's office, as if he had some business to attend to.

But Louis and Maigret waited for him to come out.

"Josaphat!" Louis called out.

"What do you want? I'm in a hurry."

"There's a gentleman here who'd like a word with you."

"Who? I'm on duty, and when I'm on duty . . ."

Maigret had the utmost difficulty steering him toward an empty spot between the storage room and the urinals.

"I just want an answer to a simple question."

The postman had his guard up, that was obvious. He pretended he heard the train, and was ready to rush off to the mail car. At the same time, he could not help glowering briefly at Louis for putting him in this position.

Maigret already knew he would get nothing out of him, that Cavre had been there before him.

"Hurry up. I can hear the train. . . ."

"About ten days ago, you called at Madame Retailleau's house to collect for a delivery."

"I'm not allowed to discuss my work."

"But you discussed it that very evening."

"In front of me!" interjected the young man. "Avrard was there, and so was Lhériteau and little Croman. . . ."

The postman shifted from one leg to the other, managing to look stupid and insolent at the same time.

"What right do you have to question me?"

"We can ask you a question, can't we? You're not the Pope, are you?"

"And what if I asked him to show me his credentials? He's been snooping around the neighborhood all morning!"

Maigret had already turned away, fully aware that it was pointless to persevere.

Louis, however, lost his temper in the face of such blatant deviousness.

"Do you mean you have the nerve to say you didn't tell everyone about the thousand-franc notes you saw in the soup tureen?"

"I can say what I like, can't I? Or are you going to try to stop me?"

"You told everyone what you saw. I'll get the others to back me up; I'll get them to repeat what you said. You even said the notes were held together by a pin."

The postman shrugged his shoulders and walked away. This time the train really was coming into the station, and he walked down the platform to where the mail car usually stopped.

"The swine!" growled Louis under his breath. "You heard what he said, didn't you? But you can take my word for it. Why should I lie? I knew perfectly well this would happen. . . ."

"Why?"

"Because it's always the same with them. . . ."

"With who?"

"With the bunch of them . . . I can't really explain. . . . They stick to-gether. . . . They're rich. . . . They're either related to magistrates or else friends of theirs. And of department heads and generals . . . I don't know whether you understand what I'm trying to say. . . . So the people are afraid. . . . They often gossip at night when they've had a bit too much to drink, and then regret it the next day.

"What are you going to do now? You're not going back to Paris, are you?"

"Of course not, son. Why do you ask?"

"I don't know. The other man looks . . ."

The young man stopped himself just in time. He was probably about to say something like:

"The other man looks so much stronger than you!"

And it was true. Through the mist that was beginning to settle, turning the light into a false dusk, Maigret thought he saw Cavre's face, his thin lips spreading into a sardonic smile.

"Isn't your boss going to be cross if you don't get back to work?"

"Oh, no! . . . He's not one of them. If he could help us prove poor Albert was murdered, he would, I promise you."

Maigret jumped when a voice behind him asked:

"How do I get to the Lion d'Or?"

The railway man on duty near the small gate pointed to the street about a hundred yards away.

"Straight ahead . . . You'll see it on your left."

A plump little man, faultlessly dressed and carrying a suitcase almost as large as himself, looked around for a nonexistent porter. The Superintendent examined him from head to foot. He had never seen him before.

—5———————

Three Women in a Living Room

Louis dived into the fog with his head bowed, and before he was enveloped completely, he said:

"If you want to get hold of me, I'll be at the Trois Mules all evening."

It was five o'clock. A thick fog had

descended, with the night, over the town. Maigret had to walk the length of the main street in Saint-Aubin to reach the station again, and then the road leading to Etienne Naud's house. Louis had offered to go with him, but there is a limit to everything, and Maigret had had enough. He was beginning to get tired of being pulled along by this overexcited, restless young man.

As they parted company, Louis, with a hint of reproach in his voice, had said feelingly:

"They'll butter you up, and you'll start believing everything they tell you." He was referring to the Nauds, of course.

With his hands in his pockets and the collar of his overcoat turned up, Maigret walked cautiously toward the light in the distance. Any lamp shining through the fog became a beacon. Because of the intense brightness of its halo, which looked as if it were still a long way off, you felt as though you were walking toward an important goal. And then, all of a sudden, he almost bumped into the cold window of the Vendée Co-operative, which he had walked past twenty times that day. The narrow shop front had been painted green fairly recently, and there were offers of free glassware and earthenware displayed in the window.

Farther on, in total darkness, he came up against something hard and groped about in confusion for some time before realizing that he had landed in the middle of the carts standing outside the wheelwright's with their shafts in the air.

Bells sounded suddenly, immediately above his head. He was walking past the church. The post office was on the right, with its doll-size counter; opposite, on the other side of the street, stood the doctor's house.

The Lion d'Or was on one side of the street, the Trois Mules on the other. It was extraordinary to think that inside each lighted house people were living in a tiny circle of warmth, like incrustations in the icy infinity of the universe.

Saint-Aubin was on a small scale. The lights in the dairy made one think of a brightly lit factory at night. At the station a locomotive with huge wheels was sending out sparks.

Albert Retailleau had grown up in this miniature world. His mother had spent all of her life in Saint-Aubin. Apart from holidays in Les Sables-d'Olonne, somebody like Geneviève Naud might never leave the town.

As the train had slowed down somewhat before it reached Niort, Maigret had noticed empty streets in the rain, rows of lights and shuttered houses. He had thought to himself:

"There are people who spend an entire lifetime in that street."

Testing the ground with his feet, he made his way along the canal toward another beacon, which turned out to be the lantern outside the Nauds' house. On cold nights or in driving rain, he had often noticed, from train windows, such isolated houses, a rectangle of yellow light, the only sign of their existence, arousing the imagination to picture all manner of things.

And now Maigret was coming into the orbit of one of these lights. He walked up the stone steps, groped for the bell, and then noticed that the door was ajar. He went into the hall, deliberately shuffling his feet to make his presence known, but this did not deter whoever was in the living room from continuing to hold forth in a monotonous tone. Maigret took off his wet overcoat, his hat, wiped his feet on the straw mat, and knocked on the door.

"Come in. . . . Geneviève, open the door."

He had already opened it. Only one of the lamps in the room was lit. Madame Naud was sewing by the fireside, and a very old woman was sitting opposite her. The young girl was walking over to the door as Maigret came into the room.

"I'm sorry to disturb you."

The girl looked at him anxiously, unable to decide whether or not he would betray her. Maigret merely bowed.

"This is my daughter, Geneviève, Superintendent. She looked forward so much to meeting you. She is quite recovered now. . . . Allow me to introduce you to my mother. . . ."

So this was Clémentine Bréjon, a La Noue before she married, and commonly known as Tine. This small, sprightly old lady, with the grimacing look one sees on busts of Voltaire, rose to her feet and asked in a curious falsetto voice:

"Well, Superintendent, do you feel you have caused enough havoc in our poor Saint-Aubin? Upon my word, I've seen you walk up and down ten times or more this morning, and this afternoon I have it on

110

good authority that you found yourself a young recruit. . . . Do you know, Louise, who acted as elephant driver to the Superintendent?"

Had she deliberately chosen the term "elephant driver" to emphasize the disproportion between the lanky youth and the elephantine Maigret?

Louise Naud, who had none of her mother's spirit and whose face was much longer and paler, did not look up from her work but just nodded her head and smiled faintly to show she was listening.

"Fillou's son . . . It was bound to happen. The boy must have lain in wait for him. . . . No doubt he has told you some pretty tall tales, Superintendent?"

"Not at all, madame . . . He merely directed me to the various persons I wanted to see. I'd have had difficulty finding their houses on my own, since the local people aren't exactly communicative."

Geneviève had sat down and was staring at Maigret as if she were hypnotized by him. Madame Naud looked up occasionally from her work and glanced furtively at her daughter.

The living room looked exactly as it had the previous evening; everything was in its

111

usual place. An oppressive stillness hung over the room. It was as if only the grandmother conveyed some sense of normality.

"I am an old woman, Superintendent. Let me tell you that some time ago, something much more serious happened, which nearly destroyed Saint-Aubin. There used to be a clog factory which employed fifty people, men and women. It was at a time when there were endless strikes in France and workers walked out on the slightest provocation."

Madame Naud had looked up from her work to listen, and Maigret saw that she found it difficult to conceal her anxiety. Her thin face bore a striking resemblance to that of Bréjon.

"One of the workmen in the clog factory was Fillou. He wasn't a bad man, but he was inclined to drink too much, and when he was tipsy he thought he was a real orator. What happened exactly? One day, he went into the manager's office to lodge a complaint of some sort. Shortly afterward the door opened. Fillou was catapulted out, staggered backward for several yards, and then fell into the canal."

"And he was the father of my young

companion with the spotty face?" inquired Maigret.

"His father, yes. He is dead now. At the time, the town was divided into two factions. One side thought that the drunken Fillou had behaved like a madman and that the manager had been forced to take violent action to get rid of him. The other side felt that it was all the manager's fault, that he had provoked Fillou, taunting him by referring to the large families of his employees with remarks like:

" 'I can't help it if they breed on Saturday nights when they're pissed. . . .' "

"Fillou is dead, you said?"

"He died two years ago of cancer of the stomach."

"Did many people support him at the time of the incident?"

"He didn't have the majority behind him, but the most fanatical people. Every morning someone else found threats written in chalk on his door."

"Are you implying, madame, that the case is similar to the one we are dealing with now?"

"I am not implying anything, Superintendent. Old people love rambling on, you know. There is always some scandal or other to discuss in small towns. Life would be very dull, otherwise. And there will always be a handful of people willing to fan the flames."

"What was the end of the Fillou affair?"

"Silence, of course."

"Yes, silence just about sums it up," thought Maigret. Despite the efforts of a small group of fanatics, silence always gets the upper hand. And he had been confronted with silence all day long.

Moreover, ever since he had come into the room, he had been in the grip of a strange feeling, a feeling that made him somewhat uneasy.

He had wandered through the streets from morning till night, sullenly and obstinately following Louis, who had passed on to him something of his own determination.

"She's one of them . . ." Louis would say.

And "them" in Louis's mind meant a number of people who had conspired not to talk, and who did not want any trouble, people who wanted to let sleeping dogs lie.

Basically, one might say, Maigret had thrown in his lot with the small group of rebels. He had had a drink with them at

114

the Trois Mules. He had disowned the Nauds by declaring that he was not working for them, and when Louis doubted his word, he was sorely tempted to give him proof of his loyalty.

And yet Louis had been justified in looking with suspicion at the Superintendent when they parted, as if he had a premonition of what would happen once his companion was again the enemy's guest. That's why he had tried to escort Maigret all the way to the Nauds' front door — to bolster him and caution him not to give in.

"If you want to get hold of me, I'll be at the Trois Mules all evening."

He would wait in vain. Now that he was back in this cozy, bourgeois living room, Maigret felt almost ashamed of himself for having wandered through the streets in the tow of a youngster and been snubbed by everyone he had persisted in questioning.

There was a portrait on the wall that Maigret had not noticed the night before, a portrait of Bréjon, the Examining Magistrate, who seemed to be staring down at the Superintendent as if to say:

"Don't forget the purpose of your visit."

He watched Louise Naud's fingers as

she sewed and was hypnotized by their nervousness. Her face remained almost serene, but her fingers revealed a fear that bordered on panic.

"What do you think of our doctor?" asked the talkative old lady. "He's a real character, isn't he? You Parisians are wrong in thinking that no one of interest lives in the country. If you were to stay here for two months, no more . . . Louise, isn't your husband coming back?"

"He telephoned a moment ago to say he will be late. He's been called to La Roche-sur-Yon. He asked me to give you his apologies, Superintendent."

"I owe you an apology, too, for not having come back for lunch."

"Geneviève! Do give the Superintendent an apéritif."

"Well, children, I must be going."

"Stay to dinner, Maman. Etienne will take you home in the car when he gets back."

"I won't hear of it, my child. I don't need anyone to drive me home."

Her daughter helped her tie the ribbons of a small black bonnet that sat jauntily on her head, and gave her galoshes to wear over her shoes.

"You are sure you don't want me to have the carriage made ready?"

"Time enough for that the day of my funeral. Good-by, Superintendent. If you're passing my house again, come in and see me. Good night, Louise. Good night, Vièvre."

And suddenly, once the door closed again, there was a sense of emptiness. Maigret understood why they had tried to make old Tine stay. Now that she had gone, a heavy, anguished silence weighed on those left behind; the room seemed to rustle with fear. Louise Naud's fingers moved ever more rapidly over her work, while the young girl tried to find an excuse for leaving the room but did not dare.

And to think that although Albert Retailleau was dead, although his mutilated body had been discovered one morning on the railroad tracks, his son was alive in this room at this very moment, in the shape of a being that would be ready to be born in a few months' time.

When Maigret turned toward the girl, she did not avoid his eyes. On the contrary, she stood up straight and looked squarely at him, as if to say:

"No, you did not dream it. I came into

your bedroom last night, and I wasn't sleepwalking. What I told you then is the truth. You can see I am not ashamed of it. I am not mad. Albert was my lover and I am expecting his child."

Albert, the son of Madame Retailleau, a woman who had stood up for her rights so bravely after her husband's death, Albert, Louis's young and fervent friend, used to creep into this house at night without anyone's knowing. And Geneviève would take him into the room, the one at the end of the right wing of the house.

"Will you excuse me, ladies? I would like to go for a short walk around the stable yards — if you have no objection, that is. . . ."

"May I come with you?"

"You'll catch cold, Geneviève."

"No, I won't, Maman. I'll wrap up warmly."

She went into the kitchen to fetch a hurricane lamp, which she brought back lit. In the hall, Maigret helped her on with her cape.

"What would you like to see?" she asked in a low voice.

"Let's go into the yard."

"We can go out this way. There's no

point in going around the house. . . . Mind the steps."

Lights were on in the stables, whose doors were open, but the fog was so thick that nothing could be seen.

"Your room is the one directly above us, isn't it?"

"Yes . . . I know what you are getting at. . . . He didn't come in through the door, naturally. . . . Come with me. . . . You see this ladder. . . . It's always left here. He just had to push it a few yards. . . ."

"Which is your parents' room?"

"Three windows along."

"And the other two windows?"

"One is the spare bedroom, where Alban slept last night. The other is a room that hasn't been used since my little sister died, and Maman has the key."

She was cold; she tried not to show it so that it would not look as if she wanted to end the conversation.

"Your mother and father had no idea?"

"No."

"Had this affair been going on for some time?"

She answered at once.

"Three and a half months."

"Was Retailleau aware of the consequence of these meetings?"

"Yes."

"What did he intend to do?"

"He was going to confess everything to my parents and marry me."

"Why was he so angry, that last evening?"

Maigret looked at her closely, trying his best to glimpse the expression on her face through the fog. The ensuing silence betrayed the young girl's amazement.

"I asked you . . ."

"I heard what you said."

"Well!"

"I don't understand. Why do you say he was angry?"

And her hands trembled like her mother's, causing the lantern to shake.

"Nothing out of the ordinary happened between you that night?"

"No, nothing."

"Did Albert leave by the window, as usual?"

"Yes . . . There was a moon. . . . I saw him go over to the back of the yard, where he could jump over the little wall onto the road."

"What time was it?"

"About half past twelve."

"Did he always stay so briefly?"

"What do you mean?"

She was playing for time. Behind a window, not far from where they were standing, they could see the old cook moving about.

"He arrived at about midnight. I imagine he usually stayed longer. . . . You didn't quarrel?"

"Why should we have quarreled?"

"I don't know. . . . I'm just asking. . . ."

"No."

"When was he to speak to your parents?"

"Soon . . . We were waiting for a propitious moment."

"Try to remember accurately. . . . Are you sure there were no lights on in the house that night? You heard no noise? There was no one skulking in the yard?"

"I didn't see anything. . . . I swear to you, Superintendent, I know nothing. . . . Maybe you don't believe me, but it's the truth. I'll never — do you hear? — never tell my father what I told you last night. . . . I shall leave. I don't yet know what I'll do. . . ."

"Why did you tell me?"

121

"I don't know. . . . I was frightened. . . . I thought you would find out everything and tell my parents."

"Shall we go back? You're shivering."

"You won't say anything?"

He did not know what to say. He did not want to be bound by a promise. He muttered:

"Trust me."

Was he, too, "one of them," to use Louis's phrase? Oh! Now he understood perfectly what the young man meant. Albert Retailleau was dead and buried. A certain number of people in Saint-Aubin — the majority, in fact — thought that since it was impossible to bring the young man back to life, the wisest course of action was to treat the subject as closed.

To be "one of them" was to belong to that tribe. Even Albert's mother was "one of them," since she had not seemed to understand why anyone would want to investigate her son's death.

And those who had not subscribed to this view at the outset had been brought to heel one after the other.

Désiré wished he had never found the cap. What cap? He now had money to drink his fill and could send a money order for five hundred francs to his good-for-nothing son.

Josaphat, the postman, could not remember having seen a wad of thousand-franc notes in the soup tureen.

Etienne Naud was embarrassed that his brother-in-law should have thought of sending someone like Maigret, a man bent on discovering the truth.

But what was the truth? And who stood to gain by discovering the truth? What good would it do?

The small group of men in the Trois Mules, a carpenter, a plowman, and a young man named Louis Fillou, whose father had already proved to be strong-willed, were the only ones to keep the affair alive.

"Aren't you hungry, Superintendent?" asked Madame Naud, when Maigret returned to the living room. "Where is my daughter?"

"She was in the hall just now. I suppose she has gone up to her room for a minute."

For the next quarter of an hour the atmosphere was gloomy indeed. Maigret and Louise Naud were now alone in the old-fashioned, stuffy room. From time to time a log toppled over and sent sparks flying in the grate. Only one lamp was lit, and its pink shade shed a soft glow over the furniture. Familiar sounds coming from the kitchen occasionally broke the silence. They could hear the stove being filled with coal, a saucepan being moved, an earthenware plate being put on the table.

Maigret sensed that Louise Naud would have liked to talk. She was possessed by a demon who was pushing her to say . . .

To say what? She was visibly tortured. Sometimes she would open her mouth, as if she had decided to speak, and Maigret was afraid of what she was going to say.

She said nothing. Her chest tightened in a nervous spasm and her shoulders shook for a second. She went on with her embroidery, making tiny stitches, weighed down by this cloak of immobility and stillness, which formed such a barrier between them.

Did she know that Retailleau and her daughter . . .

"Do you mind if I smoke, madame?"

She gave a start. Perhaps she had been afraid he was going to say something else.

She stammered:

"Please do. . . . Make yourself at home."

Then she sat up straight and listened for a sound.

"Oh, good heavens . . ."

Oh, good heavens, what? She was merely waiting for her husband to return, waiting for someone to come and end the torment of this tête-à-tête.

And then Maigret began to feel sorry for her. What was to stop him from getting up and saying:

"I think your brother made a mistake in asking me to come here. There is nothing I can do. This whole affair is none of my business, and, if you don't mind, I'll take the next train back to Paris. I am most grateful to you for your hospitality."

He recalled Louis's pale face, his fiery eyes, the sardonic smile.

But mostly he pictured Cavre, with his briefcase under his arm; Cavre, who after all these years had suddenly been given the chance to get the better of his hated former boss. For Cavre did hate him. Admittedly, he hated everyone, but he hated Maigret in particular, because Maigret was his alter ego, a successful version of his own self.

Cavre had doubtless been up to all sorts of shady tricks ever since he got off the train the night before and was nearly mistaken by Naud for Maigret himself.

Where was the clock that was going tick-tock? Maigret looked around for it. He felt really disturbed, and said to himself:

"Another five minutes and this poor woman's nerves will get the better of her. She'll make a clean breast of it. She can't stand it any longer. She's at the end of her tether."

All he had to do was ask her one specific question. Hardly that! He would go up to her and look at her searchingly. Would she be able to restrain herself then?

But instead, he remained silent and even timidly picked up a magazine that was lying on a small round table, to put her at her ease. It was a woman's magazine, full of embroidery patterns.

Just as in a dentist's waiting room one reads things one would never read anywhere else, Maigret turned the pages and looked carefully at the pink and blue pictures, but the invisible chain that bound him to his hostess remained as tight as ever.

They were saved by the entry of the maid. She was rather a rough-looking country girl, whose black dress and white apron merely accentuated her rugged, irregular features.

"Oh! Pardon . . . I didn't know there was someone . . ."

"What is it?"

"I wanted to know if I should set the table or wait for Monsieur."

"Set the table."

"Will Monsieur Alban be here for dinner?"

"I don't know. But set his place as usual. . . ."

What a relief to talk of everyday things! They were so simple and reassuring. She latched on to Alban as a topic of conversation.

"He came to lunch today. It was he who answered the telephone when you called. . . . He leads such a lonely life. We consider him one of the family now. . . ."

The maid's appearance had opened an avenue of escape, and she made the most of it.

"Will you excuse me for a moment? You know what it's like to run a house. There is always something to see to in the kitchen. . . . I'll ask the maid to tell my daughter to come down and keep you company."

"Please don't bother."

"Besides . . ." She listened carefully.

"Yes. . . . That must be my husband. . . ."

A car drew up in front of the steps, but the engine kept running. They heard voices, and Maigret wondered whether his host had brought someone back with him, but he was only giving instructions to a servant who had rushed out on hearing the car.

Naud came into the living room, still wearing his leather coat. There was an anxious look in his eyes as he surveyed Maigret and his wife, astonished to find them alone together.

"Ah! You're . . ."

"I was just saying to the Superintendent, Etienne, that I would have to leave him for a minute and see to things in the kitchen."

"Forgive me, Superintendent. . . . I am on the board of the regional agricultural authority and I had forgotten to tell you we had an important meeting today."

He sneezed and poured himself a glass of port, still trying to gauge what might have happened in his absence.

"Well, have you had a good day? I was told on the telephone you were too busy to come back for lunch."

He, too, was afraid of being alone with the Superintendent. He looked around at the armchairs in the room, as if to reproach them for being empty.

"Alban's not here yet?" he said with a forced smile, turning toward the dining-room door, which was open.

And his wife answered from the kitchen:

"He came to lunch. He didn't say whether he'd be back for dinner."

"Where's Geneviève?"

"She went up to her room."

He did not dare sit down, settle in a chair. Maigret understood how he felt and almost came to share his anxiety. In order to feel strong, or simply to control their trembling, the three of them needed to be together, side by side, in an unbroken family circle.

Only then would the Superintendent be able to sense the spirit of the house in normal times. The atmosphere of mutual support, the small talk that provided a continuous reassuring background.

"Will you have a glass of port?"

129

"I just had one."

"Well, have another. . . . Now, tell me what you've been doing. Or, rather . . . for perhaps I am being indiscreet . . ."

"The cap has disappeared," declared Maigret, his eyes on the carpet.

"Has it really? This famous cap was to be proof. . . . And where had it been? Mind you, I have always had my doubts as to whether it really existed. . . ."

"A young fellow by name of Louis Fillou claims it was in one of the drawers in his bedroom."

"In Louis's house? And you mean it was stolen? This morning? Don't you think that is rather odd?"

He stood there laughing, a tall, strong, sturdy figure of a man, with a ruddy complexion. He was the owner of this house, the head of the family, and he had just taken part in administrative duties in La Roche-sur-Yon. He was Etienne Naud — Squire Naud, as the local people would have said — the son of Sébastien Naud, a man known and respected by everyone in the district.

But his laughter sounded shaky as he took a glass of port and looked around in vain for the habitual support his family

would give him — he would have liked
them to be present, his wife, his daughter,
and even Alban, who had decided to stay
away today of all days.

"Will you have a cigar? . . . No, you
are sure?"

He paced back and forth restlessly, as
though to sit down would have been to fall
into a trap, to play right into the hands of
the formidable Superintendent, whom that
half-wit of a brother-in-law had foisted on
him. Etienne Naud felt doomed.

—6—

Alban Groult-Cotelle's Alibi

Before dinner that evening, an incident
occurred which, although insignificant in
itself, nonetheless gave Maigret food for
thought. Etienne Naud had still not sat
down, as though afraid of being even more
at the mercy of the Superintendent if he
did not move. They could hear voices in
the dining room. Madame Naud was
reprimanding the maid for not cleaning the

silver properly. Geneviève had just come downstairs.

Maigret saw the look her father gave her as she came into the room. It held a trace of anxiety. Naud had not seen his daughter since she had retired to her room the day before, saying she did not feel well. It was perfectly natural, too, that Geneviève should reassure him with a smile.

Just at that moment the telephone rang, and Naud went into the hall to answer it. He left the door open.

"What?" he said, in an astonished tone of voice. "Of course he's here, damn it. What did you say? . . . Yes, hurry up. We're expecting you."

When he came back into the living room, he was still shrugging his shoulders.

"I wonder what has got into our friend Alban. There's been a place for him at our table for years. Now he calls this evening to find out if you're here, and when I say you are, he asks if he can come to dinner and says he must talk to you. . . ."

By chance, Maigret happened to be looking, not at Naud, but at his daughter, and he was surprised to see a fierce expression on her face.

"He did the same thing earlier today,"

she said crossly. "He came here for lunch and looked very peeved when he realized the Superintendent hadn't come back. I thought he was going to leave. He muttered:

" 'What a pity. I had something to show him.'

"He took his leave as soon as he had gulped down his dessert. You must have met him in the town, Superintendent."

Whatever it was, was so subtle that Maigret could not pinpoint it. A hint of something in the girl's voice. And yet it was not really the voice. What is it, for example, that makes an experienced man suddenly realize that a young girl has become a woman?

Maigret noticed something of this sort. It seemed to him that Geneviève's peevish words conveyed something more than plain ill temper, and he decided to watch young Mademoiselle Naud more closely.

Madame Naud came in, apologizing for her absence. Her daughter took the opportunity to repeat:

"Alban has just called to say he's coming to dinner. But first of all he asked whether the Superintendent was here. He's not coming to see *us*. . . ."

"He'll be here in a minute," said her father, who had finally sat down now that his family was around him. "It will take him three minutes by bicycle."

Maigret dutifully remained seated, looking somewhat dispirited. His large eyes were expressionless, as was usual with him when he found himself in an awkward situation. He watched them in turn, responding with a half-smile when spoken to and thinking to himself:

"They must be cursing their idiot of a brother-in-law and me, too. They all know what happened, including their friend Alban. That's why they are jittery the minute they are on their own. They feel reassured when they are together and gang up. . . ."

What had happened, in fact? Had Etienne Naud discovered the young Retailleau in his daughter's bedroom? Had they quarreled? Had they had a fight? Or had Naud quite simply shot him down as he would a rabbit?

What a night to have lived through! Geneviève's mother must have been in a terrible state, and the servants, who probably heard the noise, must have been petrified.

Someone was scraping his feet at the front door. Geneviève made a move, as if to go to open the door, but then decided to remain seated, and Naud himself, somewhat taken aback, as if his daughter's behavior was a serious breach of habit, got up and went into the hall. Maigret heard him talking about the fog, and then the two men came into the room.

This was actually the first time that Maigret was seeing Geneviève and Alban together. She held out her hand rather stiffly. Alban bowed, kissed the back of her hand, and then turned toward Maigret, obviously anxious to tell him or show him something.

"Would you believe it, Superintendent? After you left this morning I came across this quite by chance. . . ."

And he held out a small sheet of paper, which had been attached to some others with a pin, for there were two tiny prick marks in it.

"What is it?" asked Naud, quite naturally, while his daughter looked distrustfully at Alban.

"You have all made fun of my mania for hoarding the smallest scrap of paper. I could produce the tiniest laundry bill dated

135

three or eight years back!"

The piece of paper that Maigret was twirling between his thick fingers was a bill from the Hôtel de l'Europe in La Roche-sur-Yon. Room: 30 francs. Breakfast: 6 francs. Service . . . The date: January 7.

"Of course," said Alban, as though he were apologizing, "it's not important. However, I remembered the police like alibis. Look at the date. Quite by chance, I was in La Roche, do you see, on the night the person you're interested in met his death. . . ."

Naud and his wife reacted as well-bred people do when confronted with a breach of manners. Unable to believe her ears, Madame Naud looked first at Alban, as though she would not have expected such behavior from him, and then looked down with a sigh at the logs in the grate. Her husband frowned. He was slower on the uptake. Perhaps he was hunting for some deeper meaning to his friend's ploy.

As for Geneviève, she had turned pale with anger. She had obviously had a real shock, and her eyes were throwing sparks. Maigret had been so intrigued by her behavior a few moments before that he tried not to look at anyone else.

The thin, lanky Alban, with his balding forehead, stood sheepishly in the middle of the room.

"Well, you're making quite sure you are in the clear without waiting to be accused," said Naud when he finally spoke, having had time to weigh his words.

"What do you mean by that, Etienne? I think you're all misreading me. I came across this hotel bill quite by chance when I was sorting out some papers. I was eager to show it to the Superintendent because it was such a strange coincidence — the same date as the day. . . ."

Madame Naud even chipped in, something that rarely happened.

"So you've already said," she retorted. "I think dinner is ready now. . . ."

The atmosphere was strained. Although the meal was as elaborate and well cooked as it had been on the previous evening, their efforts to create a friendly ambience, or, at any rate, an outward show of relaxation, failed dismally. Geneviève was the most agitated. For a long time afterward Maigret could picture her, her chest heaving with emotion: a woman's anger — but also a mistress's rage, Maigret was sure. She pecked at her food disdainfully. Not once did she look at Alban, who, for his part, made sure he caught no one's eye.

Alban was just the sort of man to keep the smallest scraps of paper and file them away, pinning them together in bundles as if they were bank notes. It was also just like him to extricate himself from a difficulty if he had the chance, and with a clear conscience leave his friends in hot water.

All this made itself felt. Something nasty had entered the atmosphere. Madame Naud's anxiety increased. Naud, on the other hand, endeavored to reassure his family, although quite probably with another objective in mind.

"By the way, I happened to meet the Public Prosecutor in Fontenay this morning. In fact, Alban, he is almost a relative of yours, on the distaff side, since he married a Deharme, from Cholet."

"The Cholet Deharmes aren't related to the General's family. They originally came from Nantes, and their . . ."

Naud went on:

"He was most reassuring, you know, Superintendent. Although he has told my brother-in-law, Bréjon, that there is bound to be an official investigation, it will be just a formality, at any rate as far as we are concerned. I told him you were here. . . ."

He immediately regretted this slip of the tongue. Blushing slightly, he hurriedly put a large piece of lobster *à la crème* into his mouth.

"What did he have to say to that?"

"He admires you greatly and has followed most of your cases in the papers. It is precisely because he admires you . . ."

The poor man did not know how to extricate himself.

"He is amazed that my brother-in-law thought it necessary to involve a man like you in such a trivial matter. . . ."

"I see."

"You're not annoyed, I hope? He said this only because of his admiration for . . ."

"Are you sure he didn't also say that my appearance here may well make the case seem more important than it actually is?"

"How did you know? Have you seen him?"

Maigret smiled. What else could he do? Was he not a guest in their house? The Nauds had entertained him as well as they could. And again, that night, the dinner they served was a consummate example of traditional provincial cooking.

In a pleasant, very polite way, his hosts now began to make him feel that his presence in their midst was a threat, a potentially harmful factor.

There was a silence, as there had been a short while before, after the Alban episode. It was Madame Naud who tried to straighten things out, and she made a bigger blunder than her husband had.

"Anyway, I hope you'll stay a few more days with us. I expect there will be a frost after the fog has gone, and you will be able to have some walks with my husband. . . . Don't you think so, Etienne?"

How relieved they all would have been if Maigret had replied, as they assumed he would, as any well-bred man would:

"I would be delighted to stay, and greatly appreciate your hospitality, but alas, I must return to my duties in Paris. I may pass this way during the holidays. . . . But I have enjoyed myself enormously. . . ."

He said nothing of the kind. He went on eating and did not reply. Inwardly, he felt like a brute. These people had behaved well toward him from the outset. Perhaps

Albert Retailleau's death weighed heavily on their consciences. But had not the young man robbed their daughter of her honor, as they put it in their circles? And had Albert's mother, Madame Retailleau, made a fuss? Or had she been the first to realize that it was far better to let sleeping dogs lie?

Three or four people, perhaps more, were trying to keep their secret, desperately trying to prevent anyone from discovering the truth, and for someone like Madame Naud, just Maigret's presence must have been an intolerable strain. Had she not been on the point of crying out in anguish a short while ago, at the end of a quarter of an hour alone with the Superintendent?

It would be so simple! He would leave the following morning, with the whole family's blessing, and back in Paris, Bréjon, the Examining Magistrate, would thank him with tears in his eyes.

And if Maigret did not leave, was it his passion for justice only that prompted him to do otherwise? He would not have dared to assert this, in an eyeball-to-eyeball confrontation. For there was Cavre. There were the successive defeats Cavre had inflicted on him ever since their arrival the night before, without so much as a glance in the direction of his former boss. He came and went as if Maigret did not exist, or as if he were a totally innocuous opponent.

In Cavre's wake, as though by magic, evidence melted away, witnesses could remember nothing or refused to speak, and items of unmistakable proof, like the cap, vanished into thin air.

At last, after so many years, the hapless, envy-stricken, wretched Cavre was having his moment of triumph!

"What are you thinking about, Superintendent?"

He gave a start.

"Nothing . . . I'm so sorry. My mind wanders sometimes. . . ."

He had helped himself to a huge plateful of food without realizing what he was doing and was now ashamed of himself. To put him at his ease, Madame Naud said quietly:

"Nothing gives the hostess more pleasure than to see her cooking appreciated. Alban eats like a wolf, so he doesn't count; he'd eat anything put in front of him. Everything tastes good to him. He's not a gourmet. He's a glutton."

She was joking, of course, but nonetheless there was a trace of spite in her voice and expression.

A few glasses of wine had heightened the color of Etienne Naud's complexion. Playing with his knife, he ventured:

"So what do you make of it all, Superintendent, now that you've seen something of the neighborhood and have asked a few questions?"

"He has met young Fillou," his wife informed him, as though in warning.

And Maigret, who was being watched by all of them as by so many hawks, said slowly and clearly:

"I think Albert Retailleau had very bad luck."

This remark was quite meaningless, and Geneviève grew pale, indeed seemed so taken aback by these few insignificant words that for a moment it appeared that she might get up and leave the room. Her father looked puzzled. Alban sneered:

"That's a statement quite worthy of the ancient oracles! I'd certainly be very uneasy if I hadn't miraculously found proof that I was sleeping peacefully in a room in the Hôtel de l'Europe five miles from here, on that very night. . . ."

"Don't you know," retorted Maigret,

"that we in the police force consider the person with the best alibi a prime suspect?"

Alban was annoyed. Taking Maigret's little joke seriously, he answered:

"If that's so, you will have to include the Prefect's private secretary among your suspects, since he spent the evening with me. He is a childhood friend of mine, and whenever we meet and spend an evening together we don't usually get to bed until two or three in the morning."

What made Maigret decide to carry on with the game? Was it the blatant cowardice of this trumped-up aristocrat that stimulated him? He took a large notebook with an elastic band around it out of his pocket and asked, in all seriousness:

"What is his name?"

"Do you really want it? As you wish . . . Musellier, Pierre Musellier . . . He's single. He has an apartment on Place Napoléon, above the Murs garages, about fifty yards from the Hôtel de l'Europe."

"Shall we have coffee in the living room?" suggested Madame Naud. "Will you serve it, Geneviève? You're not too tired? You look pale to me. Do you think you had better go upstairs to bed?"

144

"No."

She was not tired. She was tense. It was as if she had various accounts to settle with Alban. She did not take her eyes off him.

"Did you return to Saint-Aubin the following morning?" asked Maigret, with a pencil in his hand.

"The very next morning, yes. A friend gave me a lift in his car to Fontenay-le-Comte, where I had lunch with some other friends, and just as I was leaving I bumped into Etienne, who brought me back."

"You make your way from friend to friend, as it were. . . ."

He could not have made it clearer that he thought Alban a sponger, which was the truth. Everyone understood perfectly the implication of Maigret's words. Geneviève blushed and looked away.

"Are you sure you won't change your mind and have one of my cigars, Superintendent?"

"Would you be so kind as to tell me if you have finished questioning me? If you have, I would like to take my leave. I want to get home early tonight."

"That's absolutely fine. In fact, I'd like to walk as far as the town, so if it's all right with you, we can go together."

145

"I came by bicycle."

"That doesn't matter. A bicycle can be pushed by hand, can't it? And anyway, you might bicycle into the canal in this fog."

What *was* going on? For one thing, when Maigret had talked of leaving with Alban Groult-Cotelle, Etienne Naud had frowned and had looked to be on the point of accompanying them.

Was he afraid that Alban, who was far too nervous that night, might be tempted to say too much? He had given him a long look, as if to say:

"For heaven's sake, watch out! Look at the state you are in. He is tougher than you are."

Geneviève gave Alban an even sterner, more contemptuous look, which said:

"At least try to control yourself!"

Madame Naud did not look at anyone. She was worn out. She no longer understood what was going on. It would not be long before she cracked under such nervous tension.

But the person to behave most strangely was Alban himself. He made no move to leave, but wandered aimlessly around the living room, the ulterior motive in all probability being to have a private talk with Naud.

"Shouldn't we have a word in your study about that insurance matter?"

"What insurance matter?" Naud asked stupidly.

"Never mind. We'll talk about it tomorrow."

What did he want to tell Naud that was so important?

"Are you coming, my dear fellow?" persisted the Superintendent.

"Are you sure you don't want me to take you in the car? If you would like to have the car and drive yourself . . ."

"No, thank you. We'll have a good chat on the way."

The fog swirled around them. Alban pushed his bicycle with one hand and walked quickly along, constantly having to stop because Maigret would not walk more briskly.

"They are such nice people! Such a close-knit family . . . But it must be rather a dull life for a young girl, don't you think? Has she many friends?"

"Not that I know of, at least not around here . . . Every once in a while she goes off to spend a week or so with her cousins, and they come down here in the summer, but apart from that . . ."

"I imagine she also visits with the Bréjons in Paris?"

"Yes, indeed. She stayed with them this winter."

Maigret changed the subject, playing the innocent. The two men could scarcely see each other in the icy white mist that enveloped them. The electric light in the station acted as a beacon and, farther on, two more lights, which could have been boats out at sea, shone through the haze.

"So apart from staying in La Roche-sur-Yon from time to time, you hardly ever leave Saint-Aubin?"

"I sometimes go to Nantes, since I have friends there, and also to Bordeaux, where my cousin from Chièvre lives. Her husband is a ship owner."

"Do you ever go to Paris?"

"I was there a month ago."

"At the same time as Mademoiselle Naud?"

"Maybe. I'm not sure. . . ."

They walked past the two inns that faced each other. Maigret stopped and suggested:

"What about having a drink in the Lion d'Or? It would be most interesting to see my old colleague Cavre. I saw a man at the station just recently and I suspect him to have been called in as reinforcement."

"I'll take my leave, then," said Alban quickly.

"No, no . . . If you don't want to stop, I'll keep you company on your way home. You can't object to that, now, can you?"

"I am in a hurry to get back and to bed. I'll be frank with you. . . . I am prone to the most dreadful migraines, and I am in the throes of one now."

"All the more reason to escort you home. Does your maid sleep in the house?"

"Of course."

"Some people don't like their servants to be under the same roof at night. . . . Look! There's a light."

"It's the maid."

"Is she in the living room? Of course, the room is heated. . . . Does she do odd sewing jobs for you at night?"

They stopped outside the front door, and Alban, instead of knocking, hunted in his pocket for the key.

"See you tomorrow, Superintendent! No doubt we will meet at my friends the Nauds'."

"Tell me . . ."

Alban took care not to open the door, lest Maigret think he was inviting him inside.

"It's embarrassing. . . . Please forgive me. . . . But the call of nature, you know — and since we're here . . . Among men, I needn't be shy."

"Come in. . . . I'll show you the way."

Although the light was not on in the hallway, the living-room door on the left was half open and revealed a rectangle of light. Alban tried to lead Maigret down the hallway, but the Superintendent, with an almost instinctive gesture, pushed the door wide open. Then he stopped in his tracks and cried out:

"Well, I never! It's my old friend Cavre! What are you doing here, my dear fellow?"

The former inspector had risen to his feet, looking as pale and sullen as ever. He glowered at Groult-Cotelle, whom he deemed responsible for this disastrous meeting.

Alban was completely out of his depth. He tried hard to think of an explanation but, unable to do so, merely asked:

"Where is the maid?"

Old Cadaverous was the first to regain

his composure and, bowing, said:

"Monsieur Groult-Cotelle, I presume?"

Alban was slow to join in the inspector's game.

"I am sorry to disturb you at such an hour, but I just wanted a few words with you. Since your maid told me you would not be back late . . ."

"All right!" growled Maigret.

"What?" said Alban with a start.

"I said: All right!"

"What do you mean?"

"I don't mean anything. Cavre, where is this maid who showed you in? There is no other light on in the house. So she was in bed."

"She told me . . ."

"All right! I'll give it another try, and this time I don't want any claptrap. You can sit down, Cavre. . . . You made yourself comfortable; you took off your overcoat and left your hat on the coatrack. What have you been reading?"

Maigret's eyes opened wide when he inspected the book lying on a table near Cavre's chair.

"*Sexual Perversions!* Well, now! And you found this charming book in the library of our friend Groult-Cotelle. . . . Tell me, gentlemen, why don't you sit down? Does my presence disturb you? Don't forget your migraine, Monsieur Groult-Cotelle. You should take an aspirin."

In spite of everything, Alban still had enough presence of mind to retort:

"I thought you needed to relieve yourself?"

"Well, I don't any more. . . . Now, my dear Cavre, what is this investigation of yours all about? You must have been really put out when you realized I was involved in this, too, eh?"

"Ah! You're involved? How do you mean, involved?"

"So Groult-Cotelle availed himself of your expertise, did he? Far be it from me to underrate it, by the way."

"I had never even heard of Monsieur Groult-Cotelle until this morning."

"It was Etienne Naud who told you about him when you met in Fontenay-le-Comte, wasn't it?"

"Superintendent, if you wish to submit me to a formal interrogation, I would like my lawyer to be present when I answer your questions."

"In the event of your being accused of stealing a cap, for instance?"

"In that event, yes."

The light bulb cast a gray light over the room because, apart from the fact that it was of insufficient voltage for the size of the room, it was also coated with dust.

"May I perhaps be permitted to offer you something to drink?"

"Why not?" answered Maigret. "Since fate has thrown us together . . . By the way, Cavre, was it one of your men I saw just now at the station?"

"He works for me, yes."

"Reinforcement?"

"Call it what you like."

"Were you planning to settle important matters with Monsieur Groult-Cotelle tonight?"

"I wanted to ask him one or two questions."

"If you wanted to see him about his alibi, you can rest assured. He thought of everything. He even kept his bill from the Hôtel de l'Europe."

Cavre kept his nerve. He had sat down in the chair he had occupied before and, with his legs crossed and his morocco-leather briefcase on his lap, appeared to be biding his time, determined, so it seemed, to have the last word yet.

Groult-Cotelle, who had filled three glasses with Armagnac, offered him one, which he refused.

"No, thank you. I only drink water."

He had been teased a great deal about this at Police Headquarters, an unintentionally cruel thing to do, since Cavre was not abstemious by choice but because of a liver ailment.

"And what about you, Superintendent?"

"Gladly!"

They fell silent. All three men appeared to be playing a strange kind of game, such as trying to see who would be the first to break the silence. Alban had emptied his glass with one swallow and had poured himself another. He remained standing, and from time to time pushed one of the books in his library back into place if it was out of line.

"Are you aware, monsieur," Cavre said to him at last in a quiet voice, icy calm, "that you are in your own house?"

"What do you mean?"

"That as master of the house you are at liberty to entertain whomever you think fit. I would have liked to talk to you alone, not in front of the Superintendent. If you prefer his company to mine, I will be glad to take my leave and arrange a meeting for some other time."

"In short, the Inspector is politely asking you to show one of us to the door forthwith."

"Gentlemen, I don't understand what this discussion is all about. Indeed, this whole affair has nothing to do with me. I was in La Roche, as you know, when the boy died. Granted, I am a friend of the Nauds. I have been a frequent visitor to their house. In a small town like ours, one's choice of friends is limited."

"Remember Saint Peter!"

"What do you mean?"

"That if you go on like this, you will have thrice denied your friends the Nauds before sunrise — assuming, of course, the fog allows the sun to rise."

"It is all very well for you to joke. My position is a delicate one, just the same. The Nauds often invite me to their house. Etienne is my friend; I don't deny the fact. But if you ask me what happened at the Nauds' that night, I don't know. And what is more, I don't want to know. So I am the wrong person to question. That's all."

"Perhaps Mademoiselle Naud would be the best person to question, then? Incidentally, I wonder if you were aware that she was looking at you far from lovingly this evening. I got the distinct impression that she had a bone to pick with you."

"With me?"

"Especially when you handed me your hotel bill and tried with such style to save your own skin. She didn't think that was very nice, not nice at all. I would be on my guard, so that she doesn't get her own back, if I were you. . . ."

Alban forced a laugh.

"You are joking. Geneviève is a charming child who . . ."

What made Maigret suddenly decide to play his last card?

". . . who is three months pregnant," he let drop, moving closer to Alban.

"What? . . . What did you say?"

As for Cavre, he was stunned. For the first time that day, he no longer looked his confident self, and he stared at his former boss in spontaneous admiration.

"Were you unaware of the fact, Monsieur Groult-Cotelle?"

"Just what are you getting at?"

"Nothing . . . I am looking for . . . You want to know the truth, too, don't you? . . . Then we will try to find it together. . . . Cavre has already laid his hands on the bloodstained cap, which is proof enough of the crime. . . . Where is that cap, Cavre?"

The Inspector slipped deeper into his armchair and did not reply.

"I had better warn you that you will pay dearly for it if you've destroyed it. . . . And now, I have the feeling that my presence is disturbing you. . . . I will therefore take leave of you both. . . . I presume I will see you for lunch tomorrow at your friends the Nauds', Monsieur Groult-Cotelle?"

He went out of the room. As soon as he had banged the front door shut, he saw a thin figure standing close by.

"Is that you, Superintendent?"

It was young Louis. Lying in wait behind the windows of the Trois Mules, he had doubtless seen the shadowy figures of Maigret and Alban as they went past. He had followed them.

"Do you know what they are saying, what everyone is saying in the town?"

His voice was trembling with anxiety and indignation.

"People are saying that *they* have got the better of you and that you are leaving on the three o'clock train tomorrow. . . ."

And this had very nearly been the truth.

—7————————————————

The Old Postmistress

One important contributing factor must
have made Maigret more sensitive than
usual at that particular moment. Scarcely
had he walked out of Groult-Cotelle's front
door and taken a few steps in the darkness,
the fog clinging to his skin like a cold
compress, when he suddenly stopped.
Young Louis, who was walking beside
him, asked:

"What's the matter, Superintendent?"

Something had just occurred to Maigret
and he was trying to follow the thought
through. He was still mindful of the sound
of voices, blurred but noisy, coming to
him from behind the shutters of the house.
At the same time, he understood why the
young man was alarmed: Maigret had
stopped dead for no apparent reason in the
middle of the sidewalk, like a heart patient

immobilized by a sudden attack.

This had nothing to do with Maigret's current preoccupations. He did, however, make a mental note:

"Ah! So there's a cardiac in Saint-Aubin. . . ."

He was later to learn, in fact, that the old doctor had died of angina pectoris. For years the townspeople had seen him suddenly stop in the middle of the street, rooted to the spot, with his hand on his heart.

There was a violent argument going on inside the house, or at least the sound of angry voices gave that impression, but Maigret paid no attention. The spotty Louis, who thought he had discovered the cause of the Superintendent's sudden halt, listened conscientiously. The louder the voices, the harder it was to make out the words. The noise sounded exactly like a record turning off-center, because a second hole had been bored in it, and blaring out unintelligible sounds.

But it was not the argument between Inspector Cavre and Alban Groult-Cotelle that made Maigret stop in his tracks and look about him somewhat distractedly.

The minute he left the house, an idea

had come to his mind; it wasn't even an idea, but something less precise, so vague, in fact, that he was now striving to recapture the memory of it. Every now and then, an insignificant happening, usually a whiff of some scent, brings back in a split second a particular moment in life. The sensation is so vivid, so gripping, that we want to hold on to this living fragment of our past, but it vanishes almost at once and we are unable to say what had stirred our thought. And since no answer to our questions is forthcoming, we end up wondering if it was not an unconscious evocation of a dream, or — who knows? — of some previous life.

Something struck Maigret the moment the front door banged shut. He knew he was leaving behind two embarrassed and angry men. Brought together by fate that night, the two of them had one thing in common, for which there was no rational explanation, however. Cavre made one think not of a bachelor, but of a husband who has been subjected to ridicule and looks woeful and abashed. Envy oozed from every pore, and envy can make one behave as deviously as certain hidden vices.

In his heart of hearts, Maigret did not

bear him a grudge. Actually, he felt sorry for him. All through his relentless pursuit, his determination to get the better of his rival, Maigret could not help feeling pity for him, a man who, in the last analysis, was fated to be a failure.

What was the connection between Cavre and Alban? The connection that exists between two completely dissimilar yet equally sordid things. It was almost a question of color. Both men were somehow gray, greenish, bedecked with moral and material dust.

Cavre exuded hatred. Alban Groult-Cotelle exuded panic and cowardice. His whole life had been run on the principle of cowardice. His wife had left him and taken the children with her. He had made no effort to either join them or bring them back. He probably had not suffered. He had selfishly reorganized his existence. A man of humble means, he lived in other people's homes, like the cuckoo. And if some misfortune befell his friends, he was the first to let them down.

And now Maigret suddenly recalled the trifling matter that had triggered this train of thought: it was the book he had caught Cavre holding when they came into the room, one of those disgustingly salacious books that are sold under the counter in seedy shops on Faubourg Saint-Martin.

Groult-Cotelle kept such books in his country library; and Cavre had zeroed in on them instinctively!

But there had been something else, and it was this something else that the Superintendent was struggling to put his finger on. For a split second, perhaps, his mind had been lit up, as by a glaring truth, but no sooner had he realized this than the thought vanished and all that remained was a vague impression. This was why he stood motionless, like a sufferer from heart disease trying to outwit his heart.

Maigret was trying to outwit his memory. He was hoping . . .

"What is that light?" he asked.

They were standing still in the fog. A little way off, Maigret could see a large halo of white, diffuse light. He concentrated his thoughts on this material thing in order to give his intuition time to revive. He now knew the town. So where, then, was this light almost opposite Groult-Cotelle's house coming from?

"It isn't the post office, is it?"

"It's the window next door," Louis

replied. "The postmistress's window. She sleeps badly and reads novels late in the night. Hers is always the last light to be switched off in Saint-Aubin."

He was still aware of the sound of angry voices. Groult-Cotelle was shouting the loudest, like a man who obstinately refuses to listen to reason. Cavre's voice was more controlled, more commanding.

Why was Maigret strongly tempted to cross the street and press his face against the postmistress's window? She was doubtless sitting reading in her kitchen. Was it intuition? A moment afterward, the thought had gone from his mind. He knew that Louis was looking at him anxiously and impatiently as he wondered what on earth was going on in his hero's head.

What was it he had sensed as the front door closed behind him? Well . . . First of all, Paris had come to mind. . . . The books, the shops on Faubourg Saint-Martin that sell that type of book had made him think of Paris. . . . Groult-Cotelle had gone to Paris . . . and Geneviève Naud must have been there at the same time. . . .

Maigret saw again, with his mind's eye, the look on Geneviève's face when Alban had produced his alibi in such an unsavory manner. He had read there more than mere scorn. A naked woman, not a young girl, had appeared to him. . . . A mistress, suddenly aware of the baseness of . . .

He had just got to this point in his thoughts when an inkling of something else had flashed through his mind, only to vanish again, leaving a vague memory of something rather nasty.

Yes, the whole affair was decidedly different from what Maigret had initially envisaged. Up until now, he had perceived only the bourgeois view of things, had witnessed a thoroughly bourgeois family's indignation upon discovering that a penniless youth with no prospects was making love to their daughter.

Had Naud shot him in a fit of fury? It was possible. Maigret almost pitied Naud, and especially his wife, who knew what had happened. She was desperately trying to control herself and overcome her terror. For her, every minute spent alone with the Superintendent was a terrible ordeal.

But now, Etienne Naud and his wife ceased to be foremost in his mind.

What was the missing link between these thoughts? The dull, balding Alban had an alibi. Was this really just a fluke? Was it also just a fluke that he had suddenly come across that bill from the Hôtel de l'Europe?

No doubt he really had spent the night there. The Superintendent was convinced of this, although he decided to check the fact just the same.

But why had he gone to La Roche-sur-Yon on that particular night? Had the Prefect's private secretary been expecting him?

"I must find out!" grumbled Maigret to himself.

He went on looking at the dim light in the room next to the post office; he still had his tobacco pouch in one hand and his pipe, which he was too preoccupied to fill, in the other.

Albert Retailleau was angry. . . .

Who had said that? None other than his young companion, Louis, Albert's friend.

"Was he really angry?" the Superintendent suddenly asked.

"Who?"

"Your friend Albert . . . You said that when he left you that last evening . . ."

"He was extremely excited. He had several brandies before going off to meet Geneviève. . . ."

"He didn't tell you anything?"

"Wait . . . He said he probably wouldn't stay forever in this godforsaken place."

"How long had he been Mademoiselle Naud's lover?"

"I don't know. . . . Wait, though . . . They weren't lovers in midsummer. They must have started sleeping together around October."

"He wasn't in love with her before that?"

"Well, if he was, he didn't talk to her."

"Ssh . . ."

Maigret stood quite still and listened carefully. The sound of voices had died away, and now, to his astonishment, the Superintendent heard a different sound.

"It's the telephone!" he exclaimed.

He had recognized the familiar sound of country telephones. Someone was turning a handle to call the woman in the post office.

"Run and have a look through the postmistress's window. . . . You'll get there quicker than I will."

He was right. A second light went on, in the window next to the first. The postmistress had gone through a door, which was slightly ajar, into the post office.

Maigret took his time. He loathed

running anywhere. In particular, it was Louis's presence that bothered him. He wanted to maintain a certain dignity in front of the young man. He at last filled his pipe, lit it, and walked slowly across the street.

"Well?"

"I knew she would listen in to the call," whispered Louis. "The old shrew always listens. The doctor even complained to La Roche about it once, but she still goes on doing it."

They could see her through the window, a small woman dressed in black, with dark hair and an ageless face. She had one hand on an earphone and held a plug in the other. The call must have come to an end at that very moment, because she moved the plugs into different holes and walked across the room to switch off the light.

"Do you think she would let us in?"

"If you knock on the little door at the back . . . This way . . . We'll go through the yard."

They groped about in pitch darkness, edging their way past various tubs filled with washing. A cat jumped out of a garbage can.

"Mademoiselle Rinquet!" the young man called out. "Please open up for a minute."

"What is it?"

"It's me, Louis. . . . Will you open up for a minute, please?"

As soon as she had unbolted the door, Maigret stepped quickly inside, afraid she might shut it again.

"There is nothing to be afraid of, mademoiselle."

He was too tall and too bulky for the tiny postmistress's tiny kitchen, which was cluttered with embroidered tray cloths and knickknacks made of cheap china or spun glass she had bought at fairs.

"Groult-Cotelle has just made a call."

"How do you know?"

"He called his friend Naud. . . . You listened in to their conversation."

Caught in the act, she defended herself awkwardly.

"But the post office is closed, monsieur. I'm not supposed to give anyone a line after nine o'clock. I sometimes do, though, since I'm up and like to be helpful."

"What did he say?"

"Who?"

"Look, if you're not going to answer my questions, I will have to come back tomorrow, officially, and draw up a written report, which will go through proper channels. . . . Now, what did he say?"

"There were two of them on the line."

"At the same time?"

"Pretty much. Sometimes they spoke at the same time. It turned into a shouting match between the two of them, and in the end I couldn't catch what they were saying. . . . They must both have had a receiver and were obviously pushing each other out of the way in front of the telephone."

"What did they say?"

"Monsieur Groult was first:

" 'Listen, Etienne, this can't go on. The Superintendent has just left. He came face to face with your man. I'm sure he knows everything, and if you continue . . .' "

"Well?" said Maigret.

"Wait . . . The other man butted in.

" 'Hello . . . Monsieur Naud? . . . Cavre speaking . . . Of course it's a great pity you didn't manage to detain him and keep him from finding me here, but . . .'

" 'But I'm the one who is compromised,' yelled Monsieur Groult. 'I've had enough; do you hear, Etienne? Put an end to all this! Telephone your lunatic brother-in-law

169

and tell him never to meddle in our affairs again. He's this wretched Superintendent's superior, and since he's the one who sent him down here, he must call him back to Paris. . . . So I'm warning you . . . if he is at your house the next time I come around, I'll . . .'

" 'Hello! Hello!' shouted Monsieur Etienne, in a real state at the other end of the line. 'Are you still there, Monsieur Cavre? . . . Alban's got me very upset. . . . Are you sure . . .'

" 'Hello! . . . This is Cavre. . . . Will you be quiet, Monsieur Groult. . . . Let me get a word in. . . . Stop pushing me. . . . Is that you, Monsieur Naud? . . . Yes . . . Well! There is nothing to worry about provided your friend Groult-Cotelle doesn't panic and . . . What? . . . Should you call your brother-in-law? . . . I'd have advised against it a moment ago. . . . No, I'm not afraid of him.' "

The postmistress, thoroughly enjoying reporting the telephone conversation, pointed a finger at Maigret and declared:

"He meant you, didn't he? . . . So he said he wasn't afraid of you, but that, because of Groult-Cotelle, who was thoroughly unreliable . . . Ssh . . ."

170

The bell rang in the post office. The little old lady rushed next door and switched on the light.

"Hello!... What?... Galvani 17.98? I don't know.... No, there shouldn't be any delay at this time of night.... I'll call you back."

Galvani 17.98 was Bréjon's home telephone number, and Maigret recognized it at once.

He looked at his watch to see what time it was. Ten minutes to eleven. Unless he had gone to the movies or the theater with his family, the Examining Magistrate was bound to be in bed. Everyone at the Palais de Justice knew that he got up at six in the morning and studied his briefs as day broke.

The plugs went into different holes.

"Is that Niort? Can you get me Galvani 17.98? Line 3 is free? Will you connect me, please? Line 2 was awful just now.... How are you?... You're on duty all night?... What?... No, you know perfectly well I never go to bed before one in the morning.... Yes, there's fog here, too.... You can't see more than a couple of yards in front of you.... It'll be icy on the roads tomorrow

morning. . . . Hello! Paris? . . . Paris?
. . . Hello! Paris? . . . Galvani 17.98?
. . . Come on, dear. . . . Speak more
clearly. . . . I want Galvani 17.98. . . .
What? . . . It's ringing? . . . I can't hear
anything. . . . Let it go on ringing. . . .
It's urgent. . . . Yes, now there's some-
one. . . ."

She turned around, terrified, for Maigret's bulky frame towered behind her as
he stretched out a hand, ready to take the
phone at the appropriate moment.

"Monsieur Naud? . . . Hello! . . .
Monsieur Naud? . . . Yes, I'm putting you
through. . . . One moment; it's ring-
ing. . . . Hold on. . . . Galvani 17.98?
Saint-Aubin, here . . . Here's line 3. . . .
Go ahead, 3. . . ."

She did not dare protest when the
Superintendent took the headset authori-
tatively from her and placed it on his head.
She put the plug firmly in the hole.

"Hello! Is that you, Victor? . . .
What? . . ."

There was interference on the line, and
Maigret had the feeling that the Examining
Magistrate was taking the call in bed. A
moment later, in response to his brother-
in-law's name:

172

"It's Etienne. . . ."

He was probably speaking to his wife, who was lying in bed beside him.

"What? . . . There has been a new development? . . . No? . . . Yes? . . . Don't shout. . . . It's making the line vibrate. . . ."

Etienne Naud was one of those men who yell on the telephone as if they are afraid of not being heard.

"Hello! . . . Listen, Victor. . . . There's nothing new to report really, no. . . . Believe me. . . . I'll write to you, anyhow. . . . Maybe I'll come and see you in Paris in two or three days. . . ."

"Please talk more slowly. . . . Move over a bit, Marthe."

"What did you say?"

"I was telling Marthe to move over. . . . Well? . . . What's going on? The Super-intendent arrived safely, didn't he? . . . What do you think of him?"

"Yes . . . Never mind. . . . In fact, it's because of him that I am calling. . . .

"Doesn't he want to investigate the case?"

"Yes . . . But he's investigating it too thoroughly. . . . Listen, Victor, you've simply got to find a way of getting him

173

back to Paris. . . . No, I can't talk now. . . . I know the postmistress and . . ."

Maigret smiled as he watched the tiny postmistress. She was bubbling over with curiosity.

"You'll find a way, I'm sure. . . . What? It will be difficult? . . . There must be a way, somehow. . . . It's absolutely vital, I assure you. . . ."

It was not hard to picture the Examining Magistrate frowning anxiously as waves of suspicion with regard to his brother-in-law began to creep into his mind.

"It is not what you are thinking. . . . But he's poking his nose here and there, talking to everyone, and doing far more harm than good. . . . Do you see? . . . If he goes on much longer, the whole town will be in an uproar, and my position will become untenable. . . ."

"I don't know what to do."

"Aren't you on good terms with his boss?"

"Yes, I am. . . . Of course, I could ask the head of the Police Judiciaire. . . . It's a delicate matter. . . . The Superintendent will find out sooner or later. It was as a pure favor to me that he agreed to go. . . .

Do you understand?"

"Do you or don't you want to cause trouble for your niece? And she's your goddaughter, may I remind you."

"It really is a serious matter, then?"

"I have already told you. . . ."

Etienne Naud's impatience was almost palpable. Alban's panic had rubbed off on him, and the fact that Cavre had not been against calling Bréjon to get him to summon Maigret back to Paris had not exactly reassured him.

"Can't I have a word with my sister?"

"Your sister has gone to bed. . . . I'm the only one downstairs. . . ."

"What does Geneviève say?"

The Examining Magistrate was obviously beginning to falter, and so fell back on commonplace remarks.

"Is it raining in your part of the world, too?"

"I don't know!" Naud yelled back. "I don't give a damn! Do you hear? Just get that confounded Superintendent of yours out of here."

"What on earth has got into you?"

"What has got into me? If this goes on, we won't be able to stay in this place, that's all. He is poking his nose into

175

everything. He says nothing. He . . . he . . ."

"Now calm down. I'll do my best."

"When?"

"Tomorrow morning . . . I'll go and see the head of the Police Judiciaire as soon as the offices are open. But it goes against the grain, let me tell you. It's the first time in my career that . . ."

"But you will do it, won't you?"

"I've told you I will."

"A telegram would probably arrive at about noon. . . . He'll be able to take the three o'clock train. . . . Make sure the telegram arrives in time."

"Is Louise all right?"

"Yes, she's all right. . . . Good night . . . Don't forget. . . . I'll explain later. . . . And don't start imagining things, please. . . . Say good night to your wife for me."

The postmistress realized from the look on Maigret's face that the conversation was over, and she took the headset from him and moved the plugs once more.

"Hello! . . . Are you through? . . . Hello, Paris . . . How many calls? . . . Two? . . . Thank you . . . Good night, my dear."

And then she turned to the Superintendent, who was putting his hat on again and relighting his pipe:

"I could be fired for this. . . . Do you think it is true, then?"

"What?"

"What people are saying . . . I can't think that a man like Monsieur Etienne, who has everything he could possibly want to make him happy . . ."

"Good night, mademoiselle. Don't worry. I'll be very discreet."

"What did they say?"

"Nothing much. Just family news . . ."

"Are you going back to Paris?"

"Maybe . . . Yes . . . It is quite possible I'll take the train tomorrow afternoon."

Maigret was calm now. He felt like himself again. He was almost surprised to find Louis waiting for him in the kitchen, and the young man was equally surprised when he sensed the change in his hero's mood. The Superintendent paid virtually no attention to him. He treated him superciliously, perhaps even with contempt, or so thought young Louis, who was cut to the quick.

Once more, they began to make their way through the fog, which seemed to reduce the world to absurdly small proportions. As before, an occasional light shone through the gloom.

"He did it, didn't he?"

"Who? . . . Did what?"

"Naud . . . He's the one who killed Albert."

"I honestly don't know, my boy. . . . It . . ."

Maigret stopped himself in time. He was going to say:

"It doesn't matter."

Because that was what he thought, or, rather, what he felt. But he realized that a statement such as this would only shock the young man.

"What did he say?"

"Nothing much . . . Incidentally, speaking of Groult-Cotelle . . ."

They were approaching the two inns. The lights were still on, and on one side of the street faces could be seen through the window like silhouettes in a Chinese shadow play.

"Yes?"

"Has he always been a close friend of the Nauds?"

"Let me think. . . . Not always, no . . . I was a small boy at the time, you see. . . . The house has been in his family for a long time, but when I was a kid we used to go there to play. It was empty then. I remember because we got into the cellar quite a few times. One of the basement windows didn't shut properly. Monsieur Groult-Cotelle was staying with some relatives of his at the time. They have a castle in Brittany, I think. . . . When he came back here, he was married. . . . You should ask some of the older people. . . . I was six or seven then. I remember his wife had a lovely little yellow car, which she drove herself, and she often used to go off in it alone."

"Were the two on visiting terms with the Nauds?"

"No . . . I am sure they weren't. Because I remember Monsieur Groult was constantly in and out at the old doctor's, who was a widower. . . . I used to see them sitting by the window playing chess. I think it was because of his wife that he didn't see the Nauds. He was friendly with them before his marriage. He and Naud went to the same school. They used to say hello to each other in the street. I used to see them chatting on the sidewalk, but that's all."

"So it was after Madame Groult-Cotelle left . . ."

"Yes . . . About three years ago . . . Mademoiselle Naud was sixteen or seventeen years old. She was back from school. She had been at a boarding school in Niort for some years and came back home only one Sunday each month. . . . I remember that, too, because whenever you saw her during the school year, you knew it was the third Sunday in the month. . . . They became friends. . . . Monsieur Groult used to spend half his time at the Nauds'."

"Do they go on holidays together?"

"Yes. To Les Sables-d'Olonne . . . The Nauds built a house there. . . . Are you going back? . . . Don't you want to know if the detective . . ."

The young man looked back at Groult-Cotelle's house and could still see a glimmer of light filtering through the shutters. Although he dared not show it, he was somewhat disillusioned with the unorthodox way Maigret seemed to be conducting this investigation.

"What did he say when you went in?"

"Cavre? Nothing . . . No, he had nothing to say. . . . Anyway, nothing of importance."

The fact of the matter was that at that particular moment Maigret was living in a world of his own and not in the present at all. He answered his young companion abstractedly, not aware what his questions amounted to.

His colleagues at the Police Judiciaire frequently joked about his going off into one of his trances, and he also knew that this habit was gossiped about behind his back.

At such moments, Maigret seemed to puff himself up out of all proportion, to become dense and weighty, inaccessible, like someone blind and dumb, a Maigret whom an uninitiated outsider would take for a half-wit or a sloth.

"So, you're concentrating your thoughts?" said someone who prided himself on his psychological acuity.

And Maigret had replied with comic sincerity:

"I never think."

And it was almost true. For Maigret was not thinking now, as he stood in the damp, cold street. He was not following any train of thought. He made himself into a sponge, as it were.

It was Sergeant Lucas who had hit on

181

this description; he had worked with Maigret over a long period of time and knew him better than anyone.

"There comes a moment in the course of an investigation," Lucas had said, "when the boss suddenly swells up like a sponge. You'd think he was filling up."

But filling up with what? At present, for instance, he was absorbing the fog and the darkness. The village around him was not just any old village. And he was not merely someone who had been cast into these surroundings by chance.

He was, rather, like God the Father. He knew this village like the back of his hand. It was as if he had always lived here, or, better still, as if he had created the little town. He knew what went on inside all those small, low houses nestling in the darkness. He could see men and women turning in the moist warmth of their beds and he followed the thread of their dreams. A dim light in a window enabled him to see a mother, half-asleep, giving a bottle of warm milk to her infant. He felt the shooting pain of the sick woman on the corner and imagined the drowsy grocer's wife waking up with a start.

He was in the café. Men holding grubby

cards and totting up red and yellow counters were seated at the polished brown tables.

He was in Geneviève's bedroom. He was suffering with her, feeling for her pride as a woman. Doubtless, she had just lived through the most painful day of her life and might even be anxiously awaiting Maigret's return so that she could slip into his room once more.

Madame Naud was wide awake. She had gone to bed, but could not get to sleep, and in the darkness of her room she lay listening for the slightest sound in the house. She wondered why Maigret had not come back, pictured her husband cooling his heels in the living room, torn between hope after his telephone call to Bréjon and anxiety at the Superintendent's absence.

Maigret felt the warmth of the cattle in the stables, heard the mare kicking, visualized the old cook in her camisole. . . . And in Groult-Cotelle's house . . . What's that? A door was opening. Alban was leading his visitor out. How he hated him! What had he and Cavre said to each other in the dusty, stale-smelling living room after the telephone call to Naud?

The door closed again. Cavre walked quickly along, his briefcase under his arm.

He was pleased, yet displeased. After all, he had almost won the game. He had beaten Maigret. Tomorrow the Superintendent would be summoned back to Paris. But nonetheless he felt a little humiliated that he had not brought this about single-handed. Furthermore, he felt thoroughly ruffled by the Superintendent's menacing tone with regard to the whereabouts of Albert Retailleau's cap. . . .

Cavre's employee would be waiting for him at the Lion d'Or, drinking brandy to while away the time.

"Are you going back right away?" asked Louis.

"Yes, my boy . . . What else can I do?"

"You're not going to give up?"

"Give up what?"

Maigret knew them all so well! He had come across so many young men like Louis in his life, boys who were just as enthusiastic, just as naïve and at the same time crafty, attacking every difficulty head on, resolved to attain their ends no matter what.

"You'll get over it, my dear fellow," he thought. "A few years from now you will bow respectfully to a Naud or a Groult-Cotelle because you'll have understood that it's the wisest thing for the son of Fillou."

And what about Madame Retailleau, all alone in her house? She was sure carefully to have removed all the franc notes from the soup tureen. She had understood long ago. She had doubtless been as good a wife and as good a mother as they come. It was probably not that she lacked feelings, but that she had realized that feelings get you nowhere. She had resigned herself to this truth.

But she was determined to defend herself with other arms. She was determined to turn all life's misfortunes into cash. Her husband's death had secured her house and an income that allowed her to bring up and educate her son.

The death of Albert . . .

"I bet," he muttered to himself in a low voice, "she wants a little house in Niort, not in Saint-Aubin. . . . A brand-new little house, spotlessly clean, with pictures of her husband and son on the wall . . . somewhere she can live comfortably and securely in her old age."

As for Groult-Cotelle and his *Sexual Perversions* . . .

"You're walking awfully quickly, Superintendent."

185

"Are you coming back with me?"

"Do you mind?"

"Won't your mother be worried?"

"Oh, she pays no attention to me."

He said these words with a mixture of pride and regret in his voice.

Off they went, past the station, along the water-logged path bordering the canal. Old Désiré would be sleeping off his wine on his dirty straw mattress. Josaphat, the postman, was proud of himself and was no doubt reckoning what he had gained from his cleverness and cunning. . . .

Ahead of them, at the end of the path, there was a circle of light, like the moon seen through the veil of a cloud, and a large, warm, and peaceful-looking house, one of those houses that passers-by look at enviously, thinking how nice it must be to live there.

"Off you go, son. . . . We're here now."

"When will I see you again? Promise me you won't leave without . . ."

"I promise."

"You're sure you're not giving up?"

"Sure."

Alas! Maigret was not exactly thrilled at the thought of what remained to be done, and he walked up to the steps of the house with his shoulders hunched. The front door was ajar. They had left it like that so that he could get in. There was a light on in the living room.

He sighed as he took off his heavy overcoat, which the fog had made even heavier, then stood for a moment on the doormat to light his pipe.

"In we go!"

Poor Etienne had sat up waiting for him, torn between hope and a deadly anxiety. That very afternoon, Madame Naud had tormented herself in similar fashion, in the same armchair as her husband was sitting in now.

A bottle of Armagnac on a small round table looked as if it had served its purpose well.

—8—

Maigret Plays Maigret

There was nothing affected about Maigret's stance. If his shoulders were hunched and his head somewhat off-center, as if he were frozen to the marrow and bent on warming himself by the stove, it was because he was cold. He had been out in the fog for some time and had paid no attention to the temperature. With his overcoat off, he shivered and suddenly seemed aware of the icy dampness, which chilled his bones.

He felt irritable, as one does when about to come down with flu. He also felt uneasy, since he disliked the task that faced him. And he was hesitant. As he was about to enter the living room, he had suddenly thought of two diametrically opposed methods of tackling the situation, just when he had to make up his mind to come to a final decision.

It was this, rather than an attempt to live up to his reputation, that made him walk into the room looking grim, with large eyes that appeared unfocused, and the swaying gait of a bear.

He looked at nothing, yet saw everything: the glass and the bottle of Armagnac, the overly smooth hair of Etienne Naud, who said with false cheerfulness:

"Did you have a good evening, Superintendent?"

He had obviously just run a comb

through his hair. He always kept one in his pocket, since he was always conscious of his appearance. Earlier, however, while he was gloomily waiting for Maigret's return, he had probably run his shaking fingers through his hair.

Instead of replying, Maigret went over to the wall on the left and adjusted a picture that was not hanging straight. This was not affectation. He could not abide seeing a picture askew on a wall. It quite simply irritated him, and he had no wish to be irritated for such a stupid reason just when he was all set to play the detective.

It was stuffy. The smell of food still lingered in the room and mingled with the scent of the Armagnac, to which the Superintendent finally helped himself.

"There!" he sighed.

Naud jumped in surprise and anxiety at that resounding "There!" It was as if Maigret, having debated the situation in his mind, had reached a conclusion.

If the Superintendent had been at Police Headquarters or had even been officially investigating the case, he would have felt obliged, in order to put the odds on his side, to use traditional methods. But traditional methods, in this particular case, would tend to weaken Naud's resistance, to scare him and shatter his nerve by making him oscillate between hope and fear.

It was easy. Just let him get entangled in his own lies first. Then vaguely bring up the subject of the two telephone calls. And then — why not, after all? — say point-blank:

"Your friend Alban will be arrested tomorrow morning."

Not that way, however! Maigret quite simply stood leaning against the mantelpiece. The flames in the fireplace scorched his legs. Naud was sitting near him, presumably going on hoping.

"I shall leave tomorrow at three o'clock, as you wish," sighed the Superintendent at last, having puffed at his pipe two or three times in quick succession.

He pitied Naud. He felt uncomfortable facing a man approximately his own age who up to now had lived a sheltered, peaceful, upright life, and who, threatened as he was by the possibility of being shut behind prison walls for the rest of his days, was playing his last cards.

Was he going to fight, to go on lying? Maigret hoped not, just as, out of compassion, one hopes that a wounded animal, clumsily shot, will die quickly. He avoided looking at him and fixed his eyes on the carpet.

"Why do you say that, Superintendent? You know you are welcome here and that my family not only likes but respects you, as I do. . . ."

"I overheard your telephone conversation with your brother-in-law, Monsieur Naud."

He put himself in the other man's shoes. Afterward, he preferred to forget such moments as these. He hurried on:

"Furthermore, you are mistaken about me. Your brother-in-law, Bréjon, asked me as a favor to come and help you in a delicate matter. I realized at once, believe me, that he had wrongly interpreted your wishes, and that it was not help of this kind that you wanted from him. You wrote to him in a moment of panic to ask his advice. You told him about the rumors circulating but you did not admit, of course, that they were true. And he, poor man, being an honest, conscientious magistrate who works by the rules, sent you a detective to sort out the mess."

Naud struggled slowly to his feet, walked over to the small round table, and poured himself a generous glass of Armagnac. His hands were shaking. There were probably beads of sweat on his forehead, although Maigret could not see it. Even if he had not pitied the man, he would have looked the other way at this crucial moment, out of human consideration.

"If you had not called in Justin Cavre, I would have left the district immediately after our initial meeting, but his presence somehow goaded me into staying."

Naud said not a word in protest, but fiddled with his watch chain and stared at the portrait of his mother-in-law.

"Of course, since I am not here on official business, I am not accountable to anyone. So you have nothing to fear from me, Monsieur Naud, and I am in a position to talk to you all the more freely. You have just been through a hellish few weeks, haven't you? And so has your wife, for I am sure she knows all about it. . . ."

The other man still did not surrender. It had got to the point where a nod of the head, a whisper, or a flutter of the eyelids was all that was required to put an end to the suspense. After that, peace would come. He could relax. He would have nothing more to hide, no game to play.

Upstairs, his wife was probably awake, straining to hear and fretting because there was no sign of the two men's coming up to bed. And what of his daughter? Had she managed to get to sleep?

"Now, Monsieur Naud, I am going to tell you what I really think, and you will understand why I have not left without coming out with it, which, strange, though it may seem, I was on the point of doing. Listen carefully, and don't be too ready to misconstrue what I say. I have the distinct impression, the near certitude, that however guilty you may be in the death of Albert Retailleau, you are also a victim of his death. I will go further. If you have been the instrument of death, you are not primarily responsible for it."

And Maigret helped himself to a drink, in order to give the other man time to weigh his words. Because Naud remained silent, he finally looked him in the eye and forced him to look back. He asked:

"Don't you trust me?"

The result was as distressing as it was unexpected, for Naud, a man in the prime of his life, capitulated by bursting into tears. His swollen eyes brimmed with tears and his lips pouted like a child's. For a few minutes he tried to control himself, standing awkwardly in the middle of the room. Then he rushed over and leaned against the wall. Covering his face with his arms, he started to sob violently, his shoulders shaking spasmodically.

Maigret now needed only to wait. Twice, Naud tried to speak, but it was too soon; he had not regained sufficient control of himself. As if out of discretion, Maigret had sat down in front of the fire and, since he did not feel free to stir it up, as he would do at home, he rearranged the logs with a pair of tongs.

"If you like, you can tell me in your own good time what really happened, although it won't serve much purpose, because it is a simple matter to reconstruct the events of the night in question. But what followed is another matter altogether."

"What do you mean?"

Naud looked just as tall and strong, but he seemed to have lost all substance. He had the air of a child who had shot up too fast and at the age of twelve is as tall and well filled out as a fully grown man.

"Did you not suspect that something was going on between your daughter and that young man?"

"But I didn't even know him, Superintendent! I mean, I knew of his existence, because I know more or less everyone in the village, but I could not have put a name to his face. I still wonder how on earth Geneviève managed to meet him, since she virtually never left the house."

"On the night in question, you and your wife were in bed, were you not?"

"Yes . . . And another thing . . . It's ridiculous, but we'd had goose for dinner. . . ."

He clung to facts of this kind, as though by investing the truth with such intimate details he somehow made it less tragic.

"I love goose, but I find it difficult to digest. . . . At about one in the morning, I got up to take some bicarbonate of soda. . . . You know the layout of the rooms upstairs, more or less. Our bathroom is next to our bedroom, then there's a spare room, and next to that a room we never go into because . . ."

"I know. . . . The memory of a child."

"My daughter's room is at the far end of the hallway, and so it is rather isolated from the rest of the house. The two maids sleep on the floor above. . . . While I was in our bathroom, groping about in the dark

— I didn't want to wake up my wife; she'd have scolded me for being greedy — I heard the sound of voices. There was an argument going on. It did not cross my mind that the noise could be coming from my daughter's room.

"However, when I went into the hallway to find out for myself, I realized this was so. There was a light under her door, too. . . . I heard a man's voice.

"I don't know what you would have done in my place, Superintendent. . . . I don't know if you have a daughter. . . . We're still rather behind the times here in Saint-Aubin. . . . Perhaps I am particularly naïve. Geneviève is twenty. But it had never occurred to me she might hide something like this from her mother and me. . . . To think that a man . . . No! You know, even now . . . ."

He wiped his eyes and mechanically took his pack of cigarettes out of his pocket.

"I almost rushed into the room in my nightshirt. . . . I'm rather old-fashioned in that respect, too, and still wear nightshirts, and not pajamas. . . . But at the last moment I realized how ridiculous I looked and went back into the bathroom. I got dressed in the dark, and just as I was putting on my socks, I heard another noise, this time outside. Since the bathroom shutters had not been closed, I drew back the curtain. There was a moon, and I could see a man climbing down a ladder into the courtyard. . . .

"I got my shoes on somehow and rushed downstairs. . . . I am not sure, but I think I heard my wife calling:

" 'Etienne . . .'

"Have you already thought of looking at the key to the door that opens into the courtyard? . . . It's an old key, a huge one, a real hammer. . . . I would not be prepared to swear that I took it off its hook without thinking, but it wasn't a premeditated action either. It had not occurred to me to kill, and if anyone had said then . . ."

He spoke softly but in a shaky voice. To calm himself, he lit his cigarette and puffed slowly at it several times, in the manner of the condemned.

"The man went around the house and jumped over the low wall by the road. I jumped over it behind him, not thinking to stifle the sound of my footsteps. He must have heard me, but he went on walking at the same pace. When I had almost caught up with him, he turned around, and, although I could not see his face, for some reason or other I got the impression he was jeering at me.

" 'What do you want of me?' he asked in an aggressive, scornful tone of voice.

"I swear to you, Superintendent, those are moments I wish with all my heart I had never lived through. I recognized him. He was only a youngster to me, but he had just left my daughter's bedroom and now he was sneering at me. I didn't know what to do. This kind of thing doesn't happen the way you imagine. I shook him by the shoulders but couldn't find the words to express what I wanted to say.

" 'So you're angry because I'm jilting your daughter, are you! The whore! . . . You were hand in glove, weren't you?' He flung these words at me."

Naud passed his hand over his face.

"I am not sure of anything any more, Superintendent. With the best will in the world, I could not give you an exact account of what happened. He was every bit as angry as I was but more in control of himself. He was insulting me, insulting my daughter. . . . Instead of falling on his knees at my feet, as I had stupidly half imagined he would do, he was making fun of me, my wife, my whole family. He said things like:

" 'A fine family, indeed!'

"He used the most obscene language when referring to my daughter, words I cannot bring myself to repeat, and then I began to hit him. I don't know how it happened. I had the key in my hand. The youth suddenly punched me hard in the stomach, and the pain was such that I began to hit him as hard as I could. . . .

"He fell. . . .

"And then I ran away. All I wanted to do was to get back to the house. . . .

"I swear to you this is the truth. . . . My first thought was to telephone the police in Benet. . . . When I got closer to the house, I saw a light on in my daughter's room. I suddenly thought that if I told the truth . . . But you must understand. . . . I went back to where I had left him. He was dead."

"You carried him to the railroad tracks," Maigret continued, to help him bring this sorry story more quickly to an end.

"That's right."

"All by yourself?"

"Yes."

"And you returned home?"

"My wife was standing behind the door that opens onto the road. She asked in a whisper:

" 'What have you done?'

"I tried to deny it all, but she knew. There was terror and pity in the look she gave me. I went to bed feeling somewhat feverish, and she went through all my clothes in the bathroom to make sure that . . ."

"I understand."

"You may or may not believe it, but neither my wife nor I has had the courage to broach the subject with our daughter. We've never talked about it, or even once referred to it together. That's probably the hardest thing of all. It is sometimes unnerving. Our household routine is exactly the same as it was in the past, and yet all three of us know. . . ."

"And Alban?"

"I don't know how to tell you. . . . At first, I did not give him a thought. . . . Then the next day I was surprised when he didn't turn up as usual as we were about to eat. I started to talk about him, for the sake of something to say. I said:

" 'I must call Alban.'

"When I did, his maid told me he wasn't in. Yet I was certain I heard his voice when the maid answered the phone. . . .

"It became an obsession with me. . . . Why doesn't Alban come? Does Alban suspect something? . . . Stupid as it may seem, I convinced myself that he constituted the only real threat, and four days later, when he still hadn't come near us, I went over to his house.

"I wanted to know the reason for his silence. I had no intention of confiding in him, but somehow I ended up telling him everything. . . .

"I needed him. . . . You would understand why if you had been in my position. . . . He used to tell me the local gossip. He also described the funeral. . . .

"I was well aware of what people were thinking from the beginning, and another idea took root in my mind. I felt I had to atone for what I had done, and this thought never left me. . . . Don't laugh at me, I beg of you."

"I have seen a great many men like you, Monsieur Naud!"

"And did they behave as stupidly as I did? Did they, one fine day, go and see the victim's mother, like I did? In melodramatic fashion, I waited until it was dark one evening, and then paid her a visit after Groult had made sure there was no one on the road. . . . I did not tell her the brutal truth. I said what a terrible misfortune it was that she, a widow, had lost her only support. . . .

"I am not sure whether it was a devil or an angel that prompted me, Superintendent. I can still see her, white-faced and motionless, standing by the hearth with a shawl around her shoulders. I had twenty thousand-franc notes in two bundles in my pocket. I didn't know how to go about putting them on the table. I was ashamed of myself. I was . . . yes, I was ashamed of her, too. . . .

"And yet the notes passed from my pocket to the table.

" 'Each year, madame, I will make it my duty to . . .'

"And when she frowned, I hurriedly added:

" 'Unless you would rather I give you a lump sum in your name which . . .' "

He could not go on, and had such difficulty breathing that he had to pour himself another glass of Armagnac.

"There it is. . . . I was wrong not to

confess to everything at the beginning. . . . It was too late afterward. . . . Nothing has changed at home, at least on the surface. . . . I don't know how Geneviève has had the courage to go on living as if nothing had happened. There have been times when I have wondered if my imagination hasn't been playing tricks on me. . . .

"When I realized that people in the village suspected me, when I began receiving anonymous letters and found out that more had been sent to the Public Prosecutor, I wrote to my brother-in-law. It was stupid of me, because what could he do — since I had not told him the truth? One so often hears it said that magistrates have the power to cover up a scandal that I vaguely imagined Bréjon would use his authority in the same way. . . .

"Instead, he sent you down here just when I had written to a private detective agency in Paris. . . . Yes! I did that, too! I picked an address at random from newspaper advertisements! Unable to bring myself to confide in my brother-in-law, I told a total stranger everything that had happened. I simply had to be reassured. . . .

"He knew you were on your way, because

when my brother-in-law told me you were arriving, I immediately sent a telegram to Cavre's agency. We arranged to meet in Fontenay the following day. . . .

"What else do you want to know, Superintendent? . . . How you must despise me! . . . Yes, you do! . . . And I despise myself, too, I assure you. . . . Of all the criminals you have known, I bet you haven't come across one as stupid, as . . ."

Maigret smiled for the first time. Etienne Naud was sincere. There was nothing artificial about his despair. And yet, as with all criminals, to use the word he himself had just used, his attitude revealed a certain pride.

It was annoying and humiliating to have bungled being a criminal!

For a few moments, or even several minutes, Maigret sat quite still and stared down at the flames curling around the blackened logs. Etienne Naud was so disconcerted by this unexpected reaction that he was at a loss what to do and stood hesitantly in the middle of the room, unsure of his next move.

Since he had confessed to everything, since he had chosen to abase himself, he had naturally supposed that the Superintendent would show him more consideration and come morally to his aid.

Had he not sunk lower than the low? Had he not painted a pathetic picture of his own and his family's plight?

Earlier, before confessing, Naud had sensed that Maigret was already sympathetic to his case and prepared to be more so. He had counted on this.

And now, all trace of sympathy had vanished. The game was over, and the Superintendent was calmly smoking his pipe, his expression one of deep thought devoid of any sentimentality.

"What would you do in my position?" Naud ventured once more.

One look made him wonder if he had gone too far. Perhaps he had overstepped the mark, like a child who is forgiven for misbehaving and as a result of such lenient treatment becomes more demanding and tiresome than ever.

What was Maigret thinking? Naud began to suspect that his manner had merely been part of a trap. He expected him to rise to his feet, take a pair of handcuffs out of his pocket, and say the sacred words:

"In the name of the law . . ."

"I am wondering . . ."

It was Maigret who hesitated, still puffing at his pipe as he crossed and uncrossed his legs.

"I am wondering . . . yes . . . I am wondering if we couldn't telephone your friend Alban. . . . What time is it? . . . Ten minutes past midnight . . . The postmistress will probably still be up and will put us through. . . . Yes, indeed . . . If you're not too tired, Monsieur Naud, I think it would be best if we got everything over with tonight, so that I can catch my train tomorrow."

"But . . ."

He could not find the right words, or, rather, dared not say what was on the tip of his tongue:

"But isn't it all over?"

"Will you excuse me?"

Maigret walked across the room, into the hall, and turned the handle of the telephone.

"Hello . . . I am sorry to bother you, dear mademoiselle. . . . Yes, it's I. . . . Did you recognize my voice? . . . Of course not . . . No problem at all . . . Could you very kindly put me through to Monsieur Groult-Cotelle, please? . . . Let it ring loud and clear, in case he's a heavy sleeper."

Through the half-open door he saw a bewildered Etienne Naud take a large gulp of Armagnac, as though resigned to his fate. The poor man was in a terrible state and seemed to have lost all his strength and nerve.

"Monsieur Groult-Cotelle? . . . How are you? . . . You were in bed? . . . What's that? . . . You were reading in bed? . . . Yes, this is Superintendent Maigret. . . . Yes, I'm with your friend. We've been having a chat. . . . What? . . . You've got a cold? . . . That's most unfortunate. . . . Anyone would think you have guessed what I was going to say. . . . We would like you to pop over here. . . . Yes, I know it is foggy. . . . You aren't dressed? . . . Well, in that case we'll come to you. . . . We'll be around in a jiffy if we take the car. . . . What? . . . You'd rather come over here? . . . No . . . Nothing in particular . . . I am leaving tomorrow. . . . I have important business to see to in Paris. . . ."

Poor Naud understood less and less what was in Maigret's mind, and stared up at the ceiling, thinking, no doubt, that his wife could hear everything and must be thoroughly alarmed. Should he go upstairs to reassure her? But was he really in a position to do so? Maigret's behavior now made him uneasy, and he was beginning to regret having admitted to the crime.

"What did you say? . . . A quarter of an hour? . . . That's too long. Be as quick as you can. . . . See you in a few minutes. . . . Thank you."

Perhaps the Superintendent was playacting to a certain extent. Perhaps he was not really angry. Perhaps he did not want to be alone with Etienne Naud and have to wait ten minutes or a quarter of an hour in the living room with him.

"He is coming over," he announced. "He's very worried. You cannot imagine what a state my telephone call has put him in."

"But he's got no reason to . . ."

"Is that what you think?" asked Maigret simply.

Naud was more and more perplexed.

"Do you mind if I go and get a bite to eat in the kitchen? . . . Stay where you are. . . . I'll find the switch. I know where the icebox is."

He switched on the light in the kitchen.

The stove had gone out. He found a chicken leg glazed with sauce. He cut and buttered a thick slice of bread.

"Tell me . . ."

He came back into the living room smiling.

"Have you got any beer?"

"Wouldn't you rather have a glass of burgundy?"

"I'd prefer beer, but if you haven't got any . . ."

"There must be some in the cellar. I always have one or two crates brought in. But since we don't drink beer very often, I don't know if . . ."

Just as, during the saddest of deathbed scenes, the family will cease weeping for a short time in the middle of the night and have a little something to eat, so the two men, after an hour of high drama, went matter-of-factly down to the cellar.

"No . . . This is lemonade. . . . Wait a minute. . . . The beer must be under the stairs."

He was right. They went back upstairs with bottles of beer under their arms and then set about finding two large glasses. Maigret resumed munching the chicken leg, which he held between his fingers; the sauce got all over his chin.

"I wonder," he said casually, "if your friend Alban will come alone."

"What do you mean?"

"Nothing. I'm willing to bet that . . ."

There was no time to finish the wager. Someone was tapping on the front door. Etienne Naud rushed to open it. Maigret meanwhile stood calmly waiting in the middle of the room with his glass of beer in one hand and the chicken and bread in the other.

He heard low voices:

"I have taken the liberty of bringing this gentleman with me. I met him on the way over here, and he . . ."

For a second, Maigret's eyes hardened, and then, with no warning, they suddenly flickered mischievously as he called to the man outside:

"Come in, Cavre! I was expecting you. . . ."

Noise Behind the Door

An impression of a dream can remain within us for a long time, sometimes all our lives, whereas the dream itself, so we are told, only lasts a few seconds. Thus, for a moment the three men entering the room seemed to Maigret to bear no resemblance to the kind of men they actually were, or, at any rate, considered themselves to be, and it was this new image of them that was to remain so vividly in his mind in later years.

They were all more or less the same age, Maigret included. And as he observed them, each in turn, he felt rather as if he was looking at a gathering of schoolboys in their senior year.

Etienne Naud was probably just as pudgy when he took his last exams as he was now. He would have had the same sturdy physique, the same soft look about him, and would undoubtedly have been very well mannered and rather shy.

The Superintendent had met Cavre not long after he had left school, and even then he had been a loner, and an ill-tempered one at that. However hard he tried — because he took pride in his appearance then — clothes simply did not sit as well on him as on other people. He always looked shabby and badly dressed. He cut a sad figure. When he was a little boy, his mother must have been forever saying to him:

"Run along and play with the others, Justin."

And no doubt she would confide to her neighbors:

"My son never plays. It worries me a bit, from the point of view of his health. He's too clever. He never stops thinking."

As for Alban, his looks had probably changed remarkably little since he was a young man: the long, thin legs, the elongated, rather aristocratic-looking face, the long, pale hands covered with reddish hairs, the upper-class elegance. . . . He would have copied his friends' compositions, borrowed cigarettes from them, and told them dirty jokes in corners.

And now they were struggling with utmost seriousness with a matter that could send one of them to jail for life. They were mature men. Two children somewhere bore the name of Groult-Cotelle, children who perhaps harbored some of their father's vices. In the house were a wife and daughter who would probably not sleep that night. As for Cavre, he was doubtless fuming at the thought that his wife might be making the most of his absence.

Something rather curious was happening. Whereas, shortly before, Etienne had confessed his crime to Maigret without a trace of shame and had laid bare, man to man, his innermost fears, now he blushed to the very roots of his hair as he ushered the visitors into the living room, trying in vain to look unconcerned.

Was it not, actually, rather a childish fancy that caused him to blush so violently? For a few seconds, Maigret became the headmaster or teacher. Naud had been kept behind to be questioned about some misdeed and been given a reprimand. His friends were now returning to the classroom and looking at him searchingly, as if to say:

"How did you make out?"

Well, he had not made out at all well. He had not defended himself. He had wept. He now wondered if there were still traces of tears on his cheeks and eyelids.

He would have liked to boast and make them think that everything had gone smoothly. Instead, he bustled about, went into the dining room to get some glasses out of the sideboard, and then poured out the Armagnac.

Did these glimpses of a time of life when our actions and conduct are as yet unimportant inspire the Superintendent? He waited until everyone was seated, then positioned himself in the middle of the room and, looking at Cavre and Alban in turn, said firmly:

"Well, gentlemen, the game's up!"

Only at this point, and for the first time since he had become involved in this case, did he play Maigret, as was said of inspectors at the Police Judiciaire who tried to imitate the great man. With his pipe between his teeth, his hands in his pockets, and his back to the fire, he talked and growled, poked at the logs with the end of the tongs, and moved with bearlike gait from one suspect to the other, either firing questions at them or suddenly breaking off so that a disturbing silence fell over the room.

"Monsieur Naud and I have just had a long and friendly chat. I announced my intention of returning to Paris tomorrow. It was far better, was it not, before taking leave of each other, to come out with the truth, and this is what we did. Why do you jump, Monsieur Groult-Cotelle? In fact, Cavre, I must apologize for having made you come out just when you were going to bed. Yes indeed! I am the guilty one. I knew perfectly well when I called our friend Alban that he wouldn't have the guts to come here alone. I wonder why he considered my invitation to come for a chat a threat. . . . He had a detective at hand and, since there was no lawyer around, he brought along the detective. . . . Isn't that right, Groult?"

"It wasn't me who sent to Paris for him!" replied the bogus country gentleman, now stripped of his air of importance.

"I know. It wasn't you who beat the unfortunate Retailleau to death, because you just happened to be in La Roche on that night. It wasn't you who left your wife; she was the one who left you. It wasn't you who . . . In fact, you're a somewhat negative character altogether, aren't you? . . . You have never done a good deed in your life. . . ."

Alarmed at being reprimanded like this,

Groult-Cotelle called Cavre to his aid, but the detective, his leather briefcase on his lap, was looking at Maigret in a somewhat anxious fashion.

He was sufficiently well acquainted with the police, and with the boss in particular, to know that this little scene was being staged for a definite purpose and that when the meeting was over, the case would be closed.

Etienne Naud had not protested when the Superintendent had declared:

"The game's up!"

What more did Maigret want? He walked up and down, stood in front of one of the portraits, went from one door to the other, all the time keeping up a steady flow of words. It was almost as if he was improvising, and now and again Cavre began to wonder if he might not be playing for time and waiting for something to happen that he knew would happen but was taking a long time to do so.

"I am leaving tomorrow, then, as you all wish me to do, and while I am about it, I could reproach you all, and especially you, Cavre, since you know me, for not having trusted me more. You knew quite well, damn it, that I was just a guest and treated as well as any guest could be.

"What happened in this house before I arrived is none of my business. At most, one might have asked my advice. What, actually, is Naud's position? He did something most unfortunate — very unfortunate even. But did anyone come forward and complain?

"No! The young man's mother declared herself satisfied. If I may say so . . ."

And Maigret deliberately made light of his next, ominous, statement, a move that misled all three men.

"The drama in question was enacted by gentlemen, all well-bred people. There were rumors abroad, admittedly. Two or three unpleasant pieces of evidence gave cause for concern, but the diplomacy of our friend Cavre and Naud's money, combined with the liking of certain individuals for liquor, averted any possible danger. And as for the cap, which in any case would not have constituted sufficient proof, I presume Cavre took the precaution of destroying it. Isn't that right, Justin?"

Cavre jumped on hearing himself addressed by his Christian name. Everybody turned to look at him, but he said nothing.

"That, in a nutshell, is the position at

present, or, rather, our host's position. Anonymous letters are in circulation. The Public Prosecutor and the police have received some of them. There may be an official inquiry into the case. What have you advised your client, Cavre?"

"I am not a lawyer."

"How modest you are! If you want to know what I think, and this is my own personal view and not a professional opinion, for I am not a lawyer either, in a few days' time, Naud will feel the need to depart with his family. He is rich enough to sell his property and retire elsewhere, possibly abroad. . . ."

Naud let out a sigh in the form of a sob at the thought of leaving what had been his whole life until now.

"That leaves our friend Alban. . . . What do you propose to do, Monsieur Alban Groult-Cotelle?"

"You don't have to answer," Cavre hurriedly interjected on seeing him open his mouth. "I would also like to say that we are under no obligation to put up with this interrogation, which, in any case, is phony. If you knew the Superintendent as well as I do, you would realize he is taking us for a real ride, as they would say at the

218

Quai des Orfèvres. I don't know whether you have confessed, Monsieur Naud, or how the Superintendent got the truth out of you, but of one thing I am sure, and that is that my former colleague has a purpose in mind. I do not know what that purpose is, but I am telling you to be on your guard."

"Well said, Justin!"

"I did not ask for your opinion."

"Well, I am giving it anyway."

And suddenly his tone changed. For the past quarter of an hour he had been waiting for something and had been forced into all this playacting as a result, but now that something had finally happened. It was not without good reason that he had continued pacing up and down, going from the hall door to the door opening into the dining room.

Nor was it hunger or greed earlier that had caused him to go into the kitchen for some bread and a hunk of chicken. He needed to know if there was another staircase besides the one leading down into the hall. And indeed there was a second staircase, for the staff, near the kitchen.

When he telephoned Groult-Cotelle, he had talked in a very loud voice, as though unaware of the fact that two women were supposed to be asleep.

Now, there was someone behind the half-open dining-room door.

"You are right, Cavre. You are no fool, even though you are rather a sorry character. . . . I have one purpose in mind and that is — let me declare it forthwith — to prove that Naud is not the real culprit."

This statement by the Superintendent stupefied Etienne Naud more than anyone else. He had to restrain himself from crying out. As for Alban, he had turned deathly pale, and small red blotches, which Maigret had not noticed before, appeared on his forehead, as if he were prey to a sudden attack of hives — a clear proof of his inner collapse.

When he saw the rash, the Superintendent remembered how a certain rather celebrated murderer, after a twenty-eight–hour interrogation, during which he had defended himself inch by inch, had suddenly wet his pants like a frightened child. Maigret and Lucas had been conducting the interrogation, and they had sniffed, looked at each other, and realized they had the upper hand.

Alban Groult-Cotelle's hives were a similar symptom of guilt, and the Superintendent had difficulty in suppressing a smile.

"Tell me, Monsieur Groult, would you rather tell us the truth yourself, or would you like me to do it for you? Take your time before answering. Naturally, you have my permission to consult your lawyer. . . . I mean Justin Cavre. Go off into a corner, if you like, and work something out between you."

"I have nothing to say."

"So it is my job to tell Monsieur Naud, who still does not know, why Albert Retailleau was killed, is it? Because strange as it might seem, even though Etienne Naud knows the young man was killed, he has absolutely no idea *why*. . . . What were you going to say, Alban?"

"You're a liar!"

"How can you say I am a liar when I haven't said anything yet? Come now! I will put the question a different way, and it will still come to the same thing. Will you tell us why, on a certain, carefully chosen day, you suddenly felt the need to go to La Roche-sur-Yon and bring back your hotel bill with meticulous care?"

Etienne Naud still did not understand, and looked anxiously at Maigret, convinced that this line of attack would prove the Superintendent's undoing. At first he had been impressed by Maigret's manner, but now the Superintendent was rapidly going down in Naud's estimation. His animosity toward Groult-Cotelle was pointless and beginning to be thoroughly obnoxious.

It had reached the point where Naud felt he had to intervene. He was an honest fellow who disliked seeing an innocent man accused, and, as host, he would not allow one of his guests to be raked over the coals.

"I assure you, Superintendent, you are barking up the wrong tree."

"My dear fellow, I am sorry to have to disillusion you, and even sorrier that what you are about to learn is extremely unpleasant. Isn't that so, Groult?"

Groult-Cotelle had shot to his feet, and it looked as if he was going to rush at his tormentor. He had the greatest possible difficulty in restraining himself. He clenched his fists, and his whole body shook. Finally, he started toward the door, but Maigret stopped him in his tracks by simply asking, in the most natural tone:

"Are you going upstairs?"

Who would have thought, on seeing the stubborn and stolid Maigret, that he was as warm as his victim? His shirt was sticking to his back. He was listening carefully. And the truth of the matter was, he was frightened.

A few minutes before, he was convinced that Geneviève was behind the door, as he hoped. He had been thinking of her when he had telephoned Groult-Cotelle earlier, and had consequently talked in a loud voice in the hall.

"If I am right," he was thinking then, "she'll come down. . . ."

And she had come down. At all events, he had heard a faint rustling sound behind the door into the dining room, and one side of the door had moved.

It was on Geneviève's account, too, that he had addressed Groult-Cotelle in such a way a moment ago. Now he was wondering if she was still there, since he could not hear a sound. It had crossed his mind that she might have fainted, but presumably he would have heard her fall.

He was longing to look behind the half-open door, and began thinking of how he could do so.

"Are you going upstairs?" he had flung at Alban.

And Alban, who seemed no longer to care, retraced his steps and positioned himself a few inches away from his enemy.

"Just what are you insinuating? Out with it! What other slanders have you got up your sleeve? There's not a word of truth in what you are going to say, do you hear?"

"Take a look at your lawyer."

Cavre looked pitiful, indeed, for he realized that Maigret was on the right track and that his client was caught in his own web of lies.

"I don't need anyone to advise me. I don't know what you might have been told or who could have fabricated such stories, but before you say anything, I would like to state that they are untrue. If some superexcited brains have succeeded in . . ."

"You are vile, Groult."

"What?"

"I say that you are a repulsive character. I say, and I repeat, that you are the real cause of Albert Retailleau's death, and that if the laws created by men were perfect, life imprisonment would not be a harsh-enough punishment for you. In fact, it would give me great personal pleasure, though I don't often feel like this, to accompany you to the foot of the guillotine."

"Gentlemen, I call you to witness . . ."

"It was not only Retailleau you killed, but others, too."

"I killed Retailleau? . . . I? . . . You're mad, Superintendent! He's mad! He's raving mad, I swear to you! . . . Where are these people I've killed? . . . Show them to me, then, if you please. . . . Well, we're waiting, Monsieur Sherlock Holmes."

He was sneering. His agitation had reached its peak.

"There is one of them," Maigret calmly replied, pointing to Etienne Naud, who was looking increasingly bewildered.

"It seems to me he's a dead man in very good health, as the saying goes, and if all my victims . . ."

Alban had walked over to where Maigret was standing in such an arrogant manner that the Superintendent's hand automatically jerked up and came down on Alban's pale cheek with a thud.

Perhaps they were going to come to blows, grab each other by the waist and roll around on the carpet, as befitted the schoolboys the Superintendent had visualized a short while before. But the sound of a hysterical voice shrieking from the top of the stairs stopped them in their tracks.

"Etienne! Etienne! . . . Superintendent! . . . Quick! . . . Geneviève . . ."

Madame Naud came down a few more steps, amazed that no one appeared to have heard her. She had already been shouting for some minutes.

"Hurry," Maigret said to Naud. "Go up to your daughter. . . ."

And he turned to face Cavre and said in a tone that invited no reply:

"Just to make sure he doesn't escape. . . . Do you hear?"

He followed Etienne Naud up the stairs and went with him into the young girl's bedroom.

"Look . . ." moaned Madame Naud, distraught.

Geneviève was lying across her bed with her clothes on. Her eyes were half-open but had the glazed look of a sleepwalker. A vial of Veronal lay broken on the carpet where she had dropped it.

"Help me, madame. . . ."

The opiate was only just beginning to

take effect, and the girl was still half-conscious. She drew back, terrified, as the Superintendent bent down and, gripping her hard, forced open her mouth.

"Bring me some water, a lot of water, warm if possible. . . ."

"You go, Etienne. . . . In the kitchen . . ."

Poor Etienne bumped his way down the hallway and back stairs like a giddy goose.

"Don't be afraid, madame. . . . We are still in time. . . . It's my fault. I didn't think she would react like this. . . . Get me a handkerchief, a towel, anything will do."

Less than two minutes later, the girl had vomited violently. Then she sat dejectedly on the edge of her bed obediently drinking down all the water the Superintendent gave her, which made her sick all over again.

"You can telephone the doctor. He won't do much more, but to be on the safe side . . ."

Geneviève suddenly broke down and began to cry, softly but with such weariness that the tears seemed to lull her to sleep.

"I'll leave you to look after her, madame. . . . I think it is best if she rests before the doctor comes. . . . In my opinion — and unfortunately I've seen rather a lot of cases like this, believe me — the danger is over."

They could hear Naud on the telephone downstairs:

"Immediately, yes . . . It's my daughter. . . . I'll explain when you get here. . . . No . . . Come as you are — in your dressing gown, if you like. It doesn't matter."

As he passed Naud in the hall, Maigret took the letter he was holding in his hand. He had noticed it lying on Geneviève's bedside table but had not had a moment to pick it up.

Naud tried to get the letter back as soon as he had put down the receiver.

"What are you doing?" he exclaimed. "It's for her mother and me."

"I will give it back to you in a moment. . . . Go upstairs and sit with her."

"But . . ."

"It's the best place for you to be, I assure you."

And Maigret went back into the living room, carefully closing the door behind him. He held the letter in his hand and was obviously reluctant to open it.

"Well! Groult?"

"You have no right to arrest me."

"I know . . ."

"I have done nothing illegal."

This momentous word almost made Maigret think he deserved to be slapped again, but he would have had to cross the room to do so and he did not have the energy.

He toyed with the letter and hesitated before finally slitting open the mauve envelope.

"Is that letter addressed to you?" protested Groult-Cotelle.

"No, and it's not addressed to you either. . . . Geneviève wrote it before taking the overdose. . . . Would you like me to return it to her parents?"

Dear Mummy, dear Daddy,
    I love you dearly. I beg you to believe me. But I must put an end to my life. I cannot go on living any longer. Do not try to find out why, and, above all, don't ask Alban to the house any more. He . . .

"Tell me, Cavre, did he tell you the whole story while we were upstairs?"

Maigret was convinced that in his agitated state, Alban had confessed because of a desperate need to cling to someone, a man who could defend him, whose job it was to do so, provided he was paid for his services.

As Cavre lowered his head, Maigret added:

"Well, what have you got to say?"

And Groult-Cotelle, whose cowardice knew no limits, chipped in:

"She was the one who started it!"

"And she, no doubt, gave you nasty little pornographic books to read?"

"I never gave her any . . ."

"And you never showed her certain pictures I saw in your library?"

"She came across them when my back was turned."

"And no doubt you felt the need to explain them to her?"

"I am not the first man of my age to take a young girl for a mistress. . . . I didn't force her. . . . She was very much in love. . . ."

Maigret laughed derisively as he looked Alban up and down.

"And it was her idea, too, to call in Retailleau?"

"If she took another lover, that is certainly no affair of mine, you must admit. I think you have colossal nerve to blame me! Me! In front of my friend Naud, just now . . ."

"What was that?"

"In front of Naud, then, I didn't dare answer, and you had the upper hand. . . ."

A car pulled up in front of the steps. Maigret went out of the room to open the front door and said, just as if he were master of the house:

"Go straight to Geneviève's room. Hurry . . ."

Then he went back into the living room, still holding Geneviève's letter in his hand.

"It was you, Groult, who panicked when she told you she was pregnant. You're a coward and always have been. You are so afraid of life that you don't trust your own efforts and so you clutch at other people's lives. . . .

"You were going to foist that child on some poor idiot, who would then become its father. . . .

"It was such a practical solution! . . . Geneviève was to snare a young man, who would think he was sincerely loved. . . . He would be told one fine day that his

231

ardor had resulted in a pregnancy. . . .
He had only to go to her father, ask to be
forgiven on bended knees, and declare
himself willing to make amends. . . .

"And you would have gone on being her
lover, wouldn't you?

"You bastard!"

It was young Louis who had put him on
the trail, when he had said:

*"Albert was angry. . . . He had several
brandies before going off to meet her."*

And Albert's behavior toward Geneviève's father? He had been insolent. He
had used the foulest language in speaking
of Geneviève.

"How did he find out?" demanded
Maigret.

"I don't know."

"Would you rather I go and ask Geneviève?"

Groult-Cotelle shrugged his shoulders.
What difference did it make, after all?
Maigret could not pin a charge on him.

"Every morning Retailleau used to go to
the post office to collect his employers'
mail as it was being sorted. . . . He would
go behind the counter and sometimes help
to sort the letters. . . . He recognized
Geneviève's handwriting on an envelope

232

addressed to me. She had not been able to see me alone for several days, and so . . ."

"I see."

"If that hadn't happened, everything would have gone according to plan. . . . And if you hadn't meddled . . ."

Of course Albert had been angry that night, when, with the incriminating letter in his pocket, he went to see the girl who had used him so shamefully for the last time. Moreover, everyone had conspired to make a fool of him, her parents included. How could he think otherwise?

They had led him up a fine garden path, and they were still trying to deceive him. The father was even pretending to have caught him, in order to make him marry his daughter.

"How did you know he had intercepted the letter?"

"I went to the post office shortly afterward. . . . The postmistress said:

" 'Wait a minute! I thought there was a letter for you.'

"She looked everywhere. . . . I called Geneviève. . . . Then I asked the postmistress who had been there when the mail was being sorted, and I realized, I . . ."

"You realized that things had taken a

turn for the worse and you decided to go and see your friend the Prefect's private secretary, in La Roche."

"That's my business."

"What do you think, Justin?"

But Cavre did not reply.

Heavy footsteps were heard on the stairs. The door opened. Etienne Naud came in, looking spent and dejected, his large eyes full of questions he sought in vain to answer. At that very moment, Maigret dropped the letter he was holding in so clumsy a fashion that it fell on top of the logs and flared up immediately.

"What have you done?"

"I'm so sorry. . . . It doesn't really matter, since your daughter is saved and she will be able to tell you herself what she put in her letter."

Was Naud fooled? Or was he like a certain type of patient, who suspects he is not being told the truth, who believes the doctor's optimistic words only partially, or not at all, but who nonetheless longs for those words, who needs to be reassured beyond all things?

"She is much better now, isn't she?"

"She is asleep. . . . It looks as though the danger is over, thanks to your swift